"I'll walk you out, Anna."

"Oh, you don't have to do that," she said.

"I told Aunt Hypatia that I would see you out," Reeves insisted, taking her by her arm.

When they made their way into the foyer, he took both her hands in his.

"Thank you for caring about my daughter," he said, his molten gaze holding hers. "Thank you especially for spending time with her. It's made a difference."

Anna nodded.

Reeves then tucked one of her hands into the curve of his arm and stepped toward the front door.

He looked at her, his smile matching hers. For one heartstopping moment their gazes held, and she actually wondered… He leaned forward and pressed a kiss to her forehead before dropping her hand and stepping back.

He opened the front door, and she stumbled through it. "Good night."

"Good night."

He waited until she walked over to her car before closing the door behind her. Anna stood in the dark, staring up at the big silent house.

It was perhaps the best moment of her life.

Books by Arlene James

Love Inspired

**The Perfect Wedding*
**An Old-Fashioned Love*
**A Wife Worth Waiting For*
**With Baby in Mind*
To Heal a Heart
Deck the Halls
A Family to Share
Butterfly Summer
A Love So Strong
When Love Comes Home
A Mommy in Mind
***His Small-Town Girl*
***Her Small-Town Hero*
***Their Small-Town Love*
†Anna Meets Her Match

*Everyday Miracles
**Eden, OK
†Chatam House

ARLENE JAMES

says, "Camp meetings, mission work and church attendance permeate my Oklahoma childhood memories. It was a golden time, which sustains me yet. However, only as a young, widowed mother did I truly begin growing in my personal relationship with the Lord. Through adversity, He has blessed me in countless ways, one of which is a second marriage so loving and romantic it still feels like courtship!"

The author of seventy novels, Arlene James now resides outside of Dallas, Texas, with her husband. Her need to write is greater than ever, a fact that frankly amazes her, as she's been at it since the eighth grade! She loves to hear from readers and can be reached via her Web site at www.arlenejames.com.

Anna Meets Her Match

Arlene James

Published by Steeple Hill Books™

STEEPLE HILL BOOKS

ISBN-13: 978-0-373-87549-8

ANNA MEETS HER MATCH

This edition published by arrangement with Steeple Hill Books.

www.SteepleHill.com

Printed in U.S.A.

Therefore, there is now no condemnation
for those who are in Christ Jesus.
—*Romans* 8:1

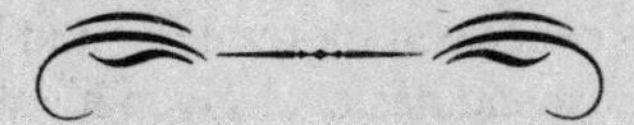

I am often asked why, after all these years,
I continue to write romance.
The answer is very simple.
I've been happily married for all this time to the
same increasingly wonderful man.
No wife has ever been more blessed in her husband,
and no husband has ever given his wife more
inspiration!
Thank you, sweetheart.
DAR

Chapter One

"Da-a-a-dy!" Gilli's muffled voice called from the backseat of the silver sedan as Reeves Leland lifted the last of the suitcases from the trunk. "Out!" Gilli demanded, rattling the disabled door handle.

He had parked the car beneath the porte cochere on the west side of the massive antebellum mansion known as Chatam House, where he and his daughter had come seeking sanctuary. "In a minute, Gilli," he said, closing the trunk lid.

Since turning three six months earlier, his daughter had grown increasingly difficult, as if he didn't have enough problems. He thought of the letter that he'd recently received from his ex-wife. The divorce had been final for nearly a year, but she had suddenly decided that he hadn't treated her fairly in the settlement. He shook his head, more pressing concerns crowding his mind. The most immediate had to do with housing.

Honeybees had driven him and his daughter out of their home. Honeybees!

Pausing in stunned contemplation Reeves felt the gray chill of an early February breeze permeate the camel-tan wool of his tailored overcoat. It rattled the dried leaves of the enormous magnolia tree on the west lawn like old bones, adding to the strangeness of the morning.

Father in heaven, I'm so confused, he thought. *Honeybees?*

Whatever God was doing in his life, he knew that he need not worry about his welcome here. He hadn't even called ahead, so certain was he of that welcome, and he gave himself a moment now to bask in that certainty, his gaze wandering over stately fluted columns, white-painted stone walls and graceful redbrick steps leading to the deep porch and the vibrant yellow, paneled side door with its so proper black framing. Terra-cotta pots flanked this side entry. In the springtime, he knew, flowers would spill over their edges, presenting a colorful welcome that would echo throughout the fifteen-acre estate.

Reeves had always loved this grand old house. The picturesque antebellum mansion and its grounds belonged to his aunts, the Chatam triplets, elder sisters of his mother. None of the aunties had ever married, but they were the first ones of whom Reeves had thought when the full weight of his situation had become clear to him.

"Da-a-dy!" Gilli bellowed.

"I'm coming. Hold on."

He took one step toward the side of the car before the sound of tires on gravel at the front of the house halted him. Turning away from his impatient daughter, he trudged to the corner of the building. A battered, foreign-made coupe pulled up at the front of the mansion. Reeves stared in appreciation at the slender blonde in dark clothing who hopped out. Lithe and energetic, with a cap of soft, wispy hair, she moved with unconscious grace. As if sensing his regard, she looked up, and shock reverberated through him. Recognizing Anna Miranda Burdett, his old childhood nemesis, Reeves frowned.

Well, that was all this day needed. Back during their

school days she had done everything in her power to make his life miserable, which was why they hadn't spoken in years, though her grandmother Tansy was a friend of his aunties. Her pranks were legendary, and he'd once had the dubious honor of being her favorite target. She'd made a travesty of his senior year, his young male pride taking a regular beating at her hands. Given his current problems, he had no patience for dealing with Anna Miranda today.

He comforted himself with the thought that she was most likely just picking up her grandmother. He couldn't imagine any other reason why she would be here at Chatam House. Hopefully, they would depart before he met with his aunts.

"Da-a-a-dy!"

He turned back toward his daughter, his footsteps crunching in the gravel as he hurried over to let her out of the car.

"I want out!" she complained, sliding down to the ground, her caramel-blond curls mingling with the fake fur on the hood of her pink nylon coat. She looked up at him, an accusing expression on her face.

A perfect combination of her mother and himself, with his rust-brown eyes and dimpled chin and Marissa's hair and winged brows, Gilli looked like every father's dream child. Unfortunately, this child whom he had wanted so much seemed terribly unhappy with him. Whatever was he going to do without Nanny?

Gilli bolted across the gravel toward the porch.

"Watch it!" he barked. Even before the warning left his mouth, she skidded and, predictably, tumbled down.

She fell to her knees, howling. Reeves reached her in two long strides and was lifting her to her feet when that yellow door opened, revealing the concerned countenance of Chester Worth. Sturdy, pale and balding, Chester and his wife, Hilda, along with her sister Carol, had served as household staff for the Chatam sisters for more than two decades. Wearing nothing more than a cardigan sweater over a plain white shirt, suspenders and slacks, Chester stepped out into the February cold, his bushy brows drawn together over his half-glasses.

Gilli's wails shut off abruptly. "H'lo, Chester," she greeted brightly.

"Miss Gilli, Mister Reeves, good to see y'all. Can I help?"

Reeves tugged Gilli forward, saying to Chester, "Could you get Gilli to the kitchen and ask Hilda to give her some lunch while I bring in the luggage?"

"Luggage, you say?" Chester asked, taking Gilli by the hand.

"We've come for a stay," Reeves replied, adding wearily, "It's been quite a morning, Chester."

"We got bees," Gilli announced, "lots and lots."

"I'll explain after I've seen the aunties," Reeves went on. "Where are they?"

"All three are in the front parlor, Mr. Reeves," Chester answered. "You just leave those bags and go let them know you're here. I'll take care of everything soon as Miss Gilli's settled. The east suite should do nicely. Bees, is it?"

"Lots and lots," Gilli confirmed.

"Thank you, Chester. I'll leave the bags inside the door."

Reeves returned to the rear of the car as the older man coaxed Gilli away. He carried the luggage into the small side entry then removed his overcoat, folding it over one arm. Smoothing his dark brown suit jacket, he headed off down a long narrow hallway, past the kitchen, butler's pantry and family parlor, toward the center of the house.

The scents of lemony furniture polish and gingerbread sparred with the musty odor of antique upholstery and the mellow perfume of aged rosewood, all familiar, all welcome and calming. Running through this house as a child with his cousins, Reeves had considered it his personal playground and more home than whichever parent's house he'd currently been living in. It had always been his one true sanctuary.

Feeling lighter than he had for some time, Reeves paused at the intersection of the "back" hall and the so-called "west" hall that flanked the magnificent curving staircase, which anchored the grand foyer at the front of the house. He lifted his eyes toward the high, pale blue ceiling, where faded feathers wafted among faint, billowy clouds framed by ornate crown moldings, and prayed silently.

It's good to be here, Lord. Maybe that's why You've allowed us to be driven from our own home. You seem to have deemed Chatam House a shelter for me in times of deepest trouble, so this must be Your way of taking care of me and Gilli. The aunties are a good influence on her, and I thank You for them and this big old house. I trust that You'll have a new nanny prepared for us by the time we go back to our place.

Wincing, he realized that he had just betrayed reluctance to be at his own home alone with his own daughter. Abruptly he felt the millstone of failure about his neck.

Forgive me for my failings, Lord, he prayed, *and please, please make me a better father. Amen.*

Turning right, Reeves walked past the formal dining room and study on one side and the quaint cloak and "withdrawing rooms" on the other, to the formal front entry, where he left his coat draped over the curved banister at the bottom of the stairs. The "east" hall, which flanked the other side of the staircase, would have taken him past the cloak and restrooms again, as well as the library and ballroom. Both of the latter received a surprising amount of use because of the many charities and clubs in which the aunties were involved. The spacious front parlor, however, was definitely the busiest room in the house. Reeves headed there, unsurprised to find the doors wide open.

He heard the aunties' voices, Hypatia's well-modulated drawl, followed by Magnolia's gruffer reply and Odelia's twitter. Just the sound of them made him smile. He paid no attention to the words themselves. Pausing to take a look inside, he swept his gaze over groupings of antique furniture, pots of well-tended plants and a wealth of bric-a-brac. Seeing none but the aunties, he relaxed and strode into the room.

Three identical pairs of light, amber-brown eyes turned his way at once. That was pretty much where the similarities ended for the casual observer, although those sweetly rounded faces, from the delicate brows, aristocratic noses, prim mouths and gently cleft chins, were very nearly interchangeable.

Hypatia, as usual, appeared the epitome of Southern gentility in her neat lilac suit with her silver hair curled into a sleek figure-eight chignon at the nape of her neck and pearls at her throat. Magnolia, on the other hand, wore a drab shirtwaist dress decades out of style beneath an oversized cardigan sweater that had undoubtedly belonged to Grandpa Hub, dead these past ten years. Her steel-gray braid hung down her back, and she wore rundown slippers rather than the rubber boots she preferred for puttering around the flowerbeds and hothouse. Lovingly referred to as "Aunt Mags" by her many nieces and nephews, she hid a tender heart beneath a gruff, mannish manner.

Odelia, affectionately but all too aptly known as Auntie Od, was all ruffles and gathers and eye-popping prints, her white hair curling softly about her ears, which currently sported enamel daisies the size of teacups. Auntie Od was known for her outlandish earrings and her sweetness. The latter imbued both her smile and her eyes as her gaze lit on the newcomer.

"Reeves!"

He could not help laughing at her delight, a patent condition for the old dear.

"Hello, Aunt Odelia." Going at once to kiss her temple, he held out a hand to Mags, who sat beside her sister on the prized Chesterfield settee that Grandma Augusta had brought back from her honeymoon trip to London back in 1932.

"Surprised to see you here this time of day," Mags stated.

Swiveling, Reeves bussed her forehead, bemused by the strength of her grip on his fingers. "Honeybees," he offered succinctly.

"What about them, dear?" Hypatia inquired calmly from her seat in the high-backed Victorian armchair facing the door through which he had entered. Its twin sat facing her, with its back to that door.

He leaned across the piecrust table to kiss her cool cheek, Mags still squeezing his hand. "They've invaded my attic."

He quickly gave them the details, how the nanny had phoned in a panic that morning, shrieking that she and Gilli were under attack by "killer bees." Racing home from his job as vice president of a national shipping company, he had found both of them locked into the nanny's car in the drive. Inside the house, a dozen or more honeybees had buzzed angrily. Nanny had climbed up on a stool to investigate a stain on the kitchen ceiling. Hearing a strange hum, she'd poked at it. Something sticky had plopped onto the counter, and bees had swarmed through the newly formed hole in the Sheetrock.

Reeves had called an exterminator, who had refused even to come out. Instead, he'd been referred to a local "bee handler," who had arrived outfitted head-to-toe in strange gear to tell him more than he'd ever wanted to know about the habits of the Texas honeybee. A quick inspection had revealed that thousands, perhaps millions, of the tiny creatures had infested his attic. It was going to take days to remove them all, and then his entire ceiling, which was saturated with honey, all of the insulation and much of the supporting structure of his roof would have to be torn out and replaced.

"Oh, my!" Odelia exclaimed, gasping. "The bees must have frightened Gilli."

He spared her a smile before turning back to Hypatia, the

undisputed authority at Chatam House. "Hardly. She wanted to know if she could keep them as pets." Gilli had been begging for a pet since her birthday, but he didn't have time to take care of a pet and so had staunchly refused.

"What can we do?" Hypatia asked, as pragmatic as ever.

"What you always do," he told her, smiling. "Provide sanctuary. I'm afraid we're moving in on you."

"Well, of course, you are," she said with a satisfied smile.

"It could be weeks," he warned, "months, even."

She waved that away with one elegant motion of her hand. She knew as well as he did that checking into a hotel with a three-year-old as rambunctious as Gilli would have been sure disaster, but he'd have chosen that option before moving in with his father, second stepmother and their daughter, his baby sister, who would soon turn four.

"There is another problem," he went on. "Nanny quit. She'd been complaining that Gilli was too much for her." Actually, she'd been complaining that he did not spend enough time with Gilli, but he was a single father with a demanding job. Besides, he paid a generous salary. "I guess the bees were the final straw. She just walked out."

"That seems to be a habit where you're concerned," drawled an unexpected voice. "Women walking out."

Reeves whirled to find a familiar figure in slim jeans and a brown turtleneck sweater slouching in the chair opposite Hypatia. A piquant face topped with a wispy fringe of medium gold bangs beamed a cheeky grin at him. His spirits dropped like a stone in a well, even as a new realization shook him. This was not the Anna Miranda of old. This Anna Miranda was a startlingly attractive version, as attractive in her way as Marissa was in hers. Oh, no, this was not the same old brat. This was worse. Much worse.

"Hello, Stick," Anna Miranda said. "You haven't changed a bit."

"I'm so sorry, dear," Hypatia cooed. "We forgot our

manners in all the excitement. Reeves, you know Anna Miranda."

Reeves frowned as if he'd just discovered the keys to his beloved first car glued to his locker door. Again. Anna smiled, remembering how she'd punished him for refusing her a ride in that car. Foolishly, she'd pined for his attention from the day that she'd first met him right here in this house soon after his parents had divorced. Even at ten, he'd had no use for an unhappy rebellious girl, especially one four years younger, and she had punished him for it, all the way through her freshman and his senior year in high school. While she'd agonized through her unrequited crush, he had pierced her hardened heart with his disdain. High school hadn't been the same after he'd graduated. Despite his coolness, she had felt oddly abandoned.

In the twelve or thirteen years since, she had caught numerous glimpses of Reeves Leland around town. Buffalo Creek simply wasn't a big enough town that they could miss each other forever. Besides, they were members of the same church, though she confined her participation to substituting occasionally in the children's Sunday school. In all those years, they had never exchanged so much as a word, and suddenly, sitting here in his aunts' parlor, she hadn't been able to bear it a moment longer.

Reeves put on a thin smile, greeting her with a flat version of the name his much younger self had often chanted in a provoking, exasperated singsong. "Anna Miranda."

Irrational hurt flashed through her, and she did the first thing that came to mind. She stuck out her tongue. He shook his head.

"Still the brat, I see."

The superior tone evoked an all too familiar urge in her. To counter it, she grinned and crossed her legs, wagging a booted foot. "Better that than a humorless stick-in-the-mud, if you ask me."

"Has anyone ever?" he retorted. "Asked your opinion, I mean."

His response stinging, she let her gaze drop away nonchalantly, but Reeves had always been able to read her to a certain extent.

"Sorry," he muttered.

Before Anna had to say anything, Odelia chirped in with a reply to Reeves's tacky question. "Why, yes, of course," Odelia declared gaily, waving a lace hanky she'd produced from somewhere. "We were just asking Anna Miranda's opinion on the announcements for the spring scholarship auction. Weren't we, sisters?"

"Invitations," Hypatia corrected pointedly. "An announcement implies that we are compelling attendance rather than soliciting it."

Anna's mouth quirked up at one corner. As if the Chatam triplets did not command Buffalo Creek society, such society as a city of thirty thousand residents could provide, anyway. With Dallas just forty-five miles to the north, Buffalo Creek's once great cotton center had disappeared, reducing the city to little more than a bedroom community of the greater Dallas/Fort Worth Metroplex. Yet, the city retained enough of its unique culture to bear pride in it, and as a daughter of the area's wealthiest family Hypatia Chatam, while personally one of the humblest individuals Anna had ever known, bore that community pride especially well.

"This spring," Hypatia said with a slight tilt of her head, "instead of holding the dinner and auction at the college, as in years past, we are opening the house instead."

This seemed no surprise to Reeves. "Ah."

Everyone knew that Buffalo Creek Bible College, or BCBC, was one of his aunts' favorite charities. Every spring, they underwrote a dinner and silent auction to raise scholarship funds. This year the event was to acquire a somewhat higher tone, moving from the drafty library hall at BCBC to the Chatam House ballroom. In keeping with the intended elegance of the occasion, they had contacted the only privately owned print shop in town for help with the necessary printed paper goods. Anna just happened to work at the print shop. Given her grandmother's friendship with the Chatam triplets, they had requested that Anna call upon them. Her boss Dennis had grudgingly allowed it.

"Anna Miranda is helping us figure out what we need printed," Mags explained. "You know, invitations, menus, advertisements…"

"Oh, and bid sheets," Hypatia said to Anna Miranda, one slender, manicured forefinger popping up.

Anna Miranda sat forward, asking, "Have you thought of printed napkins and coasters? Those might add a nice touch."

"Hmm." Hypatia tapped the cleft in her Chatam chin.

Reeves looked at Anna Miranda. "What are you, a paper salesman, er, person?"

She tried to fry him with her glare. "I am a graphic artist, for your information."

"Huh." He said it as if he couldn't believe she had an ounce of talent for anything.

"We'll go with linen napkins," Hypatia decided, sending Reeves a quelling look.

He bowed his head, a tiny muscle flexing in the hollow of his jaw.

"Magnolia, remember to tell Hilda to speak to the caterer about the linens, will you, dear?" Hypatia went on.

"If I don't do it now I'll just forget," Magnolia complained, heaving herself up off the settee. She patted Reeves affectionately on the shoulder, reaching far up to do so, as she lumbered from the room. Suddenly Anna felt conspicuously out of place in the midst of this loving family.

"I should be going, too," she said, clutching her leather-bound notebook as she rose. "If I'm not back in the shop soon, Dennis will think I'm goofing off."

Hypatia stood, a study in dignity and grace. She smiled warmly at Anna Miranda. Reeves stepped away, taking up a spot in front of the plastered fireplace on the far wall where even now a modern gas jet sponsored a cheery, warming flame.

"I'll see you out," Hypatia said to Anna, and they moved toward the foyer. "Thank you for coming by. The college press is just too busy to accommodate us this year."

"Well, their loss is our gain," Anna replied cheerfully. "I should have some estimates for you soon. Say, have you thought about creating a logo design for the fund-raiser? I could come up with something unique for it."

"What a lovely idea," Hypatia said, nodding as they strolled side by side toward the front door. "I'll discuss that with my sisters."

"Great."

Anna picked up her coat from the long, narrow, marble-topped table occupying one wall of the opulent foyer and shrugged into it. She glanced back toward the parlor and caught sight of Reeves. Frowning thoughtfully, he seemed very alone in that moment. Instantly Anna regretted that crack about women abandoning him.

As usual, she'd spoken without thinking, purely from pique because he'd so effectively ignored her to that point. It was as if they were teenagers again, so when he'd made that remark about the nanny walking out, Anna had put that together with what she'd heard about his ex simply hopping onto the back of a motorcycle and splitting town with her boyfriend. Now Anna wished she hadn't thrown that up to him. Now that the harm was done.

Reeves leaned a shoulder against the mantle, watching as Hypatia waved farewell to Anna Miranda. He didn't like what was happening here, didn't trust Anna Miranda to give this matter the attention and importance that it deserved. In fact, he wouldn't put it past her to turn this into some huge joke at his aunts' expense. He still smarted inwardly from that opening salvo, but while she could make cracks about him all she wanted, he would not put up with her wielding her malicious sense of humor against his beloved aunties. He decided to stop in at the print shop and have a private chat with her.

"Lovely. Just lovely," Odelia said from the settee, snagging his attention. "What color is it, do you think?"

"I beg your pardon?"

"Antique gold. Yes, that's it. Antique gold." She made a swirling motion around her plump face with the lace hanky. "I wish I could wear mine that short."

Reeves felt at a loss, but then he often did with Auntie Od. Adding Anna Miranda to the mix hadn't helped. He walked toward the settee. "What about antique gold?"

The hanky swirled again. "Anna Miranda's hair. Wouldn't you say that perfectly describes the color of Anna Miranda's hair?"

Antique gold. Yes, he supposed that did describe the color of Anna Miranda's short, lustrous hair. It used to be lighter, he recalled, the brassy color of newly minted gold. She'd worn it cropped at chin length as a girl. Now it seemed darker, richer, as if burnished with age, and the style seemed at once wistful and sophisticated.

Unfortunately, while she'd changed on the outside—in some rather interesting ways, he admitted—she appeared not to have done so on the inside. She seemed to be the same cheeky brat who had tried to make his life one long joke. Reeves's thoughtful gaze went back to the foyer door, through which Hypatia returned just that instant.

"She's so very lovely," Odelia prattled on, "and such a sweet girl, too, no matter what Tansy says."

"Tansy would do better to say less all around, I think," Hypatia remarked, "but then we are not to judge." She lowered herself into her chair once more and smiled up at Reeves. “Honeybees,” she said. “I’ve never heard of such a thing.”

He shrugged. “According to the bee handler, we humans and the true killer bees coming up from the south are driving the poor honeybees out of their natural habitat, so they’re adapting by invading every quiet, sheltered space they can find, including attics, hollow walls, even abandoned cars.”

The sisters traded looks. Odelia said what they were both thinking.

“We should have Chester check out the house.”

“I think, according to what the bee handler told me, the attics here would be too high for them,” Reeves assured her.

“We’ll have Chester check, just to be sure,” Hypatia decided.

A crash sounded from the depths of the great old house, followed by a familiar wail, distant and faint but audible. Reeves sighed. “I’ll start looking for another nanny tomorrow.”

Hypatia smiled sympathetically. “It’s all right, dear. I’m sure we’ll manage until you’re ready to go back to your own home.”

Reeves closed his eyes with relief. Finding another nanny was one difficult, time-consuming chore he would gladly put on the back burner for now. He had enough to contend with. He wondered if he should contact his lawyer about Marissa. Just then Mags trundled into the room, huffing for breath.

“No harm done, but Gilli’s not apt to calm down until you go to her.”

Nodding grimly, Reeves strode from the room and headed for the kitchen. The sobs grew louder with every step, but it was a sound Reeves knew only too well. Not hurt and not frightened, rather they were demanding sobs, willful sobs, angry sobs and as hopeless as any tears could ever be. Deep down, even Gilli knew that he could do nothing. He could not make Marissa love them. He could not mend their broken family.

God help us both, he prayed. But perhaps He already had, honeybees and all.

The sanctuary of Chatam House, along with the wise, loving support of the aunties, was the best thing that had happened to them in more than a year. Pray God that it would be enough to help them, finally, find their way

"Poor Reeves," Odelia said as his hurried footsteps faded.

"Poor Gilli," Mags snorted. "That boy is deaf, dumb and blind where she's concerned, though he means well, I'm sure."

"Yes, of course," Hypatia said, her gaze seeing back through the years. "Reeves always means well, but how could he know what to do with Gilli? Children learn by example, and while I love our baby sister, Dorinda hasn't always done best by her oldest two. And that says nothing of their father."

"Melinda has done well," Odelia pointed out, referring to Reeves's one full sibling. He had five half siblings, including twin sisters and a brother, all younger than him.

"True," Hypatia acknowledged, "but I wonder if Melinda's happy marriage hasn't made Reeves's divorce more difficult for him. He's a man of faith, though, and he loves his daughter. He'll learn to deal with Gilli eventually."

Mags arched an eyebrow. "What that man needs is someone to help him understand what Gilli's going through and how to handle her."

"If anyone can understand Gilli, it's Anna Miranda," Odelia gushed.

Hypatia's eyes widened. "You're exactly right about that, dear." She tapped the small cleft in her chin. Everyone in the family had one to some degree, but Hypatia wasn't thinking of that now. She was thinking of Anna Miranda's childhood.

"I believe," she said, eyes narrowing, "that Anna Miranda is going to be even more help to us than we'd assumed and in more ways than we'd realized."

Mags sat up straight, both brows rising. After a moment, she slowly grinned. Odelia, however, frowned in puzzlement.

"Do you think she'll volunteer for one of the committees?" Odelia asked.

"Oh, I think her talents are best used with the printing," Hypatia mused. "She's suggested that the fund-raiser should have its own unique logo, and I concur, but designing it will probably require a good deal of her time. After all, we have to pick just the right design."

"Exactly the right design," Magnolia agreed.

"Yes," Hypatia went on, smiling broadly, "I do think that best suits our needs."

"Ours," Magnolia purred suggestively, "and Reeves's."

"And Gilli's!" Odelia added brightly, finally seeing the wisdom of this decision.

Hypatia smiled. How perfect was the timing of God and how mysterious His ways. Honeybees, indeed.

Chapter Two

The back door of the shop had barely closed behind Anna before her boss's voice assaulted her ear. "Took you long enough!"

Dropping her notebook on the front counter, she turned toward his open office door. "I'll skip lunch to make up for the time."

She'd been late to work that morning. It happened all too frequently, despite her best efforts, and Dennis despised tardiness. He rose from behind his desk and stalked around it, his big belly leading the way. Looking down his nose at her, his sandy brown mustache quivered with suppressed anger. Her coworker Howard gave her a pitying shake of his graying head before turning back to his task. Dragging up a smile, Anna faced her employer with more aplomb than she truly felt, but that was the story of her life. She had made an art of putting up the careless, heedless front while inwardly cringing.

"They want a lot of stuff," she told him cheerfully, "and they're interested in a special logo, something unique to the fund-raiser. I'll just draw up some designs and get together some estimates."

"They better be good," Dennis warned.

"Of course," she quipped. "Good is my middle name. Isn't that why you keep me around?"

"Miranda is your middle name," he pointed out, shaking his head in confusion.

Howard sent her a chiding look. He was right. Dennis was the most sadly humorless man she'd ever known. All attempts at levity were lost on him.

The chime that signaled the opening of the front door sounded. Smile in place, Anna turned to greet a potential customer, only to freeze. Correction. Dennis was the second most humorless man she'd ever known.

"Well, if it isn't Reeves Leland." Twice in an hour's time. Some day this was turning out to be. She bucked up her smile and tossed off a flippant line. "Playing errand boy for your aunties?"

"Something like that." Reeves opened the front of his tan wool overcoat, revealing the expensive suit that clearly marked him as executive material.

Howard shook his head and turned away, as if to say she'd blundered again. Anna admired Howard. Despite his thickset build, he appeared fit for a man nearing sixty. He and his wife were devoted to one another and led quiet, settled lives, the sort that Anna could never seem to manage. Her parents had died just months after her birth in a drug-fueled automobile accident, leaving her to the oppressive care of her grandmother. Anna had rebelled early against Tansy's overbearing control, and at twenty-six, she continued to do so.

"Can I help you?" Dennis asked Reeves, elbowing Anna out of the way as he bellied up to the counter.

Reeves barely glanced at the big, blustery man. "Thank you, no. I need to speak to Anna Miranda. About my aunts and the BCBC fund-raiser."

Trembling inwardly, Anna pulled out her most professional demeanor. Reeves Leland had come to speak with her, and she couldn't imagine that was good. *Please, God,* she prayed silently, *don't let him be here to cancel the order.* Dennis would blame her for certain. She waved toward her desk around the corner. Whatever Reeves wanted, it was best dealt with in private.

"Take a seat."

She tucked her notepad under one arm and followed. Reeves glanced around at the illustrations pinned to the walls, his expression just shy of forbidding. *Be still my foolish heart,* she thought. But it was no joke. To her disgust, Reeves Leland, with his sinewy strength, cleft chin and dark hair, still had the power to send her pulse racing.

Dropping her notebook on the desk, Anna parked her hands at her waist and cut to the chase. "What's up?"

Reeves just looked at her before folding himself down onto the thinly padded steel-framed chair beside her utilitarian desk. He made himself comfortable, stretching out his long legs and crossing his ankles. All righty then. She'd play. Pulling out her armless chair, she turned it sideways and sat down, facing him.

"Okay. First guess. You're going to pay the print costs for the fund-raiser. Sky's the limit, right? Oh, joy," she deadpanned, waving her hands. "My job's secure."

"Is that what you're trying to do," he asked, "secure your job at my aunt's expense?"

She blinked at that. "Hey. They called us. I didn't call them."

Reeves folded his hands over his belt buckle, appearing to relax. "Okay, so maybe you didn't solicit their business, but that doesn't mean you don't have a secret agenda."

"Like what?"

"You tell me."

Suddenly angry, she snapped her fingers. "I never could pull anything over on you, could I, Stick? After all these years I've finally found a way to get you back for not asking me to the homecoming dance."

Ack! Had she said that out loud? It wasn't as if she'd ever actually expected him to ask her to the homecoming dance. But she'd hoped. Oh, how she'd hoped. Not that he'd believe it. He smiled thinly and sat forward, one forearm braced against the corner of her desk.

"I'm warning you, Anna Miranda," he rumbled in a low voice. "You better not make my aunts the object of one of your pranks."

Pranks? Anna goggled. She hadn't pulled a prank in years, since high school, at least. She'd been much too busy trying to feed and house herself.

"And to think," she hissed, "that I was feeling sorry for that crack I made. I heard about your wife, how she took off, and I felt bad about saying women made a habit of leaving you. Now I'm thinking maybe they got it right."

The color drained from his face. For an instant, raw pain dulled his copper-brown gaze, and once more regret slammed her. "Reeves, I'm sorry. I didn't mean that."

"My aunts," he said in a strangled voice, climbing to his feet. "I'm watching you, Anna Miranda Burdett. If you hurt or disappoint them..." Shaking his head, he started to turn away.

Desperate to convince him of her sincere regret, she reached for his arm. They jerked apart as if zapped by electricity.

"Never," she vowed, gazing up at him repentantly, her tingling hand clenched at her side. "I would never hurt your aunts. They've always been kind to me. I have the greatest respect for them, and I'll give them my very best work. You have my word."

"I haven't always found your word trustworthy," he reminded her quietly, "like the day you swore you hadn't seen my keys."

Anna flushed. "Oh, that."

What was it with men and their precious cars? She'd been

fourteen, for pity's sake, just a kid caught in the throes of an unrequited crush. She wasn't about to apologize for something that had happened twelve years ago.

Reeves nodded sharply. "Yeah, that." After staring at her for several seconds, he whirled and strode away.

Anna slumped against her chair, feeling more alone than usual, though why that should be the case, she couldn't say. She'd always been alone, after all. Obviously, that was how God intended her to be. But at least she could show Reeves Leland that he was wrong about some things. She did have talent, and she wasn't afraid to use it.

As she'd promised Reeves, she would give the Chatams her very best effort, if for no other reason than to secure her job. She'd only been here a few months. After a long string of pointless, temporary positions, she'd finally found work that she enjoyed, even if the boss was difficult. She would hate to lose that, especially since her grandmother expected her to. Also because she had to pay the rent.

The tiny one-bedroom apartment where she had lived since the age of eighteen in no way compared to the two-story, gingerbread-Victorian house where she had grown up, but Anna would crawl across glass on a daily basis to keep from moving back in with Tansy. She would do worse, she realized suddenly, to raise Reeves Leland's poor opinion of her, and that's exactly what she feared she would do. Worse.

Nevertheless, for the remainder of the week, she concentrated on showing up for work early and giving the BCBC job her best. She contacted the university and got permission to incorporate their insignia into her designs, then she experimented with fonts, illustrations and document styles until she had a handful of satisfactory possibilities to offer for consideration, along with detailed estimates for those items already discussed. She was ready by midmorning on the following Monday to meet with Reeve's aunts once again. Dennis elected to make the call informing them of that. Afterward, he told her that she had a four o'clock appointment at Chatam House. She blinked as Dennis shook a finger in her face.

"And don't think you're going to cut out at five o'clock, either. You stay until those old ladies are satisfied, or I'll wash my hands of you!"

"Be easier to wash me out of your hair," Anna quipped, eyeing the thin strands covering his poor crown. The instant the words were out, she wished them back. Dennis literally snarled at her until she muttered, "Sorry. Won't let you down. Promise."

Dennis turned away, leaving Anna to ponder whether Reeves would be there or if he would, as in years past, go out of his way to avoid her. He'd said he would be watching, but she didn't take that literally, especially as he'd shown such a marked disdain for her company. It shouldn't have bothered her so much—she had made a career, after all, of earning disapproval, especially that of her grandmother—but Reeves Leland's attitude had always wounded her. Only when she was tweaking that handsome, aristocratic nose of his had he deigned to look her way. Even then, he had only seen "the brat." Apparently that was all he saw now, too.

What hurt most was that he had always seemed unfailingly polite and kind to everyone else. Indeed, Reeves Leland had a reputation for being a fine Christian man, which was why the town had been so shocked when his wife had left him.

Pushing him out of mind, she concentrated instead on getting through the day. Howard, the dear, made sure that she got away from the office in plenty of time for her appointment. In fact, when she pulled up in front of Chatam House the dashboard clock of her old car told her that she had nearly ten minutes to spare.

Gathering her materials, she stepped out into the cold February air, tucking her chin into the rainbow-striped muffler wound about her throat inside the collar of her bright orange corduroy coat. The instant she straightened a whirling dervish came out of nowhere and knocked her on her behind. Anna instinctively put out a hand and grabbed hold. Simultaneously Carol Petty, one of the Chatams' household staff, huffed into view, her dark slacks and bulky sweater dusted with white powder, her light brown hair slipping free of the clasp at her nape. While Carol gasped for breath, the little tornado who had knocked Anna down screeched.

"Gilli Leland, stop it!" Carol scolded, stomping forward across the deep gravel to take hold of the girl. "You are going to have a bath, and that's that."

Anna hauled herself to her feet and picked up her portfolio, thankful she'd had the foresight to zip it closed as that was not always the case. Dusting off her jeans, she turned to take in the girl who had flattened her.

So this was Reeves Leland's daughter. Pretty little thing, with all that curly hair, provided one disregarded the wailing and white powder. What was that stuff covering her anyway? Talcum? Chancing a sniff, Anna leaned forward, only to draw back in surprise. The kid had coated herself in flour. Hopefully, no one planned to pan fry her, though given Carol's exasperation, Anna wouldn't have been surprised.

"I wanna make cookies!" the girl sobbed.

"Hilda is saving the cookies until you get cleaned up," Carol told the distraught child. She cast an apologetic look at Anna. "I'm sorry, Miss Burdett. A mishap in the kitchen. The misses are expecting you."

"Uh-huh, and Mr. Leland?" Anna glanced around, expecting Reeves to arrive at any moment to take his wayward offspring in hand.

Carol shook her head. "He's not in from work yet." Glancing at Gilli, she muttered, "Works too much, if you ask me."

"Hmm. Well. I'll, uh, just ring the bell, I guess."

"If you don't mind," Carol said, dragging Gilli back the way they had come.

Gilli stopped howling long enough to glance back at Anna, who impulsively stuck out her tongue and crossed her eyes. Gilli first looked surprised, but then she giggled, causing Carol to pause and look down at her. Grinning, Anna climbed the shallow brick steps and rang the bell. Odelia let her in, swinging black onyx chandeliers from her earlobes and chattering gaily about how excited they all were to see her designs.

Excited they might have been, but see her designs they did not. Neither were they interested in her estimates. Instead, Hypatia presented her with a "more complete list," of the items they would be needing: place cards, menu cards, table assignment cards, letterheads, donation forms, receipts, a spiral-bound auction catalog, name tags, item tags, signs… The list seemed endless.

While Anna tried to take in the expanding size of the order, the sisters chatted about their various ideas for the final logo design, all three at the same time. Anna mentally tossed everything she'd done to this point and quickly jotted down ideas as the sisters shot them to her. At one point she put her hand to her hair, just trying to take it all in. Hypatia reached over then to lay her manicured hand on Anna's shoulder.

"How would it be," Hypatia asked, "if you worked up designs for each of us?"

"Using your individual ideas, you mean?" Anna raised a mental eyebrow at Miss Magnolia's "nature" theme, Miss Odelia's "lace and satin" and Miss Hypatia's "biblical" motif. "I can do that." Along with a new idea of her own, she decided, suddenly picturing the fluted, Roman Doric columns of Chatam House topped with an elegant swag of flowers intertwined with the BCBC emblem, which itself contained a Bible.

"You just let us know when you're ready to meet again," Mags said. "We'll have the teapot simmering."

"That's very nice of you," Anna returned, a thought occurring. "So you'll be wanting me to continue coming *here?*"

"Is there a problem with that?" Hypatia asked.

"No, no. Not so far as I'm concerned. Dennis may not always go for it, though."

Hypatia just smiled. "Oh, he seems perfectly willing to indulge three old ladies who like their creature comforts too well."

Anna laughed. "Well, I certainly can't argue that the print shop compares in any way to Chatam House."

"What does?" a smooth male voiced asked.

Anna looked up as Reeves strolled into the room, dispensing kisses and smiles on everyone but her. At last, he turned a cool nod in her direction. "Anna Miranda."

Anna grit her teeth. She hated her full name. Hated it. Sometimes the chants of children's voices rang in her dreams. *Anna Miranda the brat. Anna Miranda the brat…*

She couldn't blame them really. They'd had parents and siblings, and she had resented that fact greatly. Of course, as children do, they had picked up on her envy. Accordingly, they had sneered, and she had made their lives miserable in every way she could imagine. Eventually she'd learned to channel her animosity into jokes, earning herself a few friends and the designation of class clown. Reeves had never thought her the least bit funny, though. She faced him and returned his greeting in kind.

"Reeves Kyle."

He lifted an eyebrow before turning his back on her. "More printing?" he asked his aunts.

Anna bit her tongue, literally.

While the aunts gushed about everything they had discussed, Anna secured her notes, reminding herself that this was business between her and the Chatam sisters. Reeves's opinion did not matter, and she had been foolish to think for a moment that it did. Or that it might ever change.

* * *

"Aunt Hypatia," Reeves asked, having listened carefully for some minutes, "are you certain that this printer is the right one for the job?"

He'd thought about it a lot. Actually, to be completely honest with himself, he'd thought about Anna Miranda, almost constantly. For some reason, he couldn't seem to get her off his mind. He kept picturing her contrite face as she'd made her apology last week, and somehow he now felt in the wrong.

She'd always done that to him. She made his life miserable and one way or another he always felt to blame. How did she do that, and why did she have to turn up again after all these years? What was God trying to tell him? That his life could be worse? That was exactly what he was trying to avoid and not just for himself. Having seen the print shop and knowing his aunts' expansive plans, Reeves truly felt that they would be better off taking their business elsewhere. Yet, because of one thing or another—primarily the complaining e-mails he'd been receiving daily from Marissa—he'd put off making the argument until now.

Hypatia smiled her serene smile, the one that could make a troubled ten-year-old feel that all might actually one day be right with his world, and answered him. "Absolutely certain. Why do you ask, dear?"

Why? Because he didn't trust Anna Miranda. No matter what she said, there would surely be a shocking message buried in a letterhead or something else inappropriate. His aunts had always defended her, however, telling him that he didn't understand her situation. The opposite seemed true to him. At least she hadn't shuttled back and forth between her warring parents throughout her childhood as he had, never quite belonging either place. Maybe her grandmother, Tansy, was a bit difficult and not the warmest person, but at least she'd provided Anna Miranda with a stable home.

"A larger shop would be better able to handle a job this size," he argued, "and with Dallas just up the road—"

"In other words, you think our shop will do shoddy work," Anna interrupted hotly. "Or is it just *my* abilities that you doubt?"

Reeves clenched his jaw. He had studiously avoided making eye contact with her, but now he leveled a stare at her face. "I didn't say that. I just don't want my aunts to be embarrassed. This scholarship fund is important to them."

Odelia laughed, her pendulous earrings wriggling. "Oh, sweetie," she chuckled. "We're embarrassed all the time."

"Not that Anna Miranda has or would embarrass us," Mags put in quickly.

"Anna Miranda is a very gifted artist, Reeves," Hypatia told him, "and she's a very dear girl."

Very dear? Not the Anna Miranda he remembered. And no girl, either, he thought, not anymore. How, he wondered, did she manage to appear so casually polished and smirk at the same time? She looked…womanly, innately female, right down to that twisted little smile.

"Besides," Anna Miranda said, "there are a surprising number of items needed, but not so many copies of each that a larger printer would find it worthwhile."

Reeves opened his mouth to argue with that, but just then Gilli came sliding into the room in her stocking feet, her hair wet, her T-shirt and pants twisted.

"Daddy, I had a aksident and Carol made me take a bath!" she complained.

Automatically, he demanded, "What did you do?"

Mags and Auntie Od reached out to Gilli, clucking and quickly righting her clothes, while Hypatia explained that they'd had a little incident involving homemade cookies and an open bag of flour. Groaning inwardly, Reeves folded his arms.

"And just how did that bag of flour tip over, Gilli?"

Poking out her bottom lip, Gilli shrugged. "I don't know."

He doubted that, but she just stood there staring up at him with those wide eyes. Anna cleared her throat. Suddenly mortified that she, of all people, should witness this, Reeves made a snap decision. His daughter would not lack discipline as Anna Miranda evidently had. He would not have a brat of his own.

"Go to your room, Gilli," he ordered, "and do not come out again until you're called down for dinner." Wailing, Gilli tore out of the parlor. Avoiding all gazes, especially Anna's, Reeves said, "I apologize. I'll make sure she's in her room, then I think I'll go out for a run."

"We'll keep an eye on her," Magnolia offered gently.

"Try to enjoy your run, dear," Ophelia told him, pity in her voice.

Some days his runs were all he did enjoy. Casting around a wan smile, Reeves strode out after his daughter. Tonight, he desperately wanted to run away from his troubles. Of late, those troubles all seemed female in nature. First Marissa had reminded him that she held joint custody of their daughter in a veiled attempted to make him renegotiate their divorce settlement. Then he returned to his one sanctuary to find Anna Miranda there and Gilli upsetting the household. All together, it was enough to add miles to his regular routine.

Of all his problems, however, Anna Miranda was the one he couldn't get off his mind. She had once seemed intent on making his life miserable, and now she was at it again. He knew, as he had known even way back in school, that the best way to deal with her was to ignore her. Unfortunately, he didn't seem able to do it now, which made no sense at all.

Then again, what in his life did?

The aunts exchanged worried glances as they settled for evening prayers.

Odelia pulled her hot pink robe tighter as she snuggled

into the corner of the well-used sofa. Several dozen pink foam curlers covered her head. "It's too bad Reeves had to work this evening," she commented sadly. "Gilli missed him."

Reeves had returned from his run with only enough time to hurriedly shower before sliding into his seat at the dinner table. After the meal, he'd spent the evening in his room on his laptop, while Gilli played glumly in the shared private sitting room of the aunties' suite. Grumpy and sullen, the child had whined and fussed until Reeves had come and taken her off to bed. It had become painfully obvious that Reeves avoided the child, which was why she acted out.

"Remind you of anyone?" Hypatia asked from her chair beside the fireplace.

"Just Anna Miranda," Mags said, dropping down beside Odelia.

"Oh, but Tansy didn't ignore Anna Miranda," Odelia protested.

Mags snorted. "She criticized her daylight to dark, you mean."

"Do you remember that time Tansy scolded little Anna Miranda for plucking roses off her front bushes?" Odelia asked with a giggle.

Hypatia nodded, a smile tugging at her lips. "As I recall, Anna Miranda used a pair of sewing scissors to snip off every one of Tansy's prized blossoms. The result was a bumper crop the next year."

All three chuckled, but then Mags sobered. "If anyone can understand Gilli, it is Anna Miranda," she insisted.

"Well, it's certainly not Reeves," Hypatia said with a sigh. "I've tried speaking to him about it myself a time or two, but he always seems so hurt by the slightest criticism." They all knew who was responsible for that. Marissa had destroyed Reeves's hard-won self-esteem. "I suppose we must simply pray that God will somehow reach him."

Was it possible, she wondered silently, that Anna Miranda might be God's tool in this? Might she be the one to help Reeves stop hiding his heart and learn how to deal with his little girl? It occurred to her suddenly that their Heavenly Father might have something more in mind than they had yet considered.

"Oh, sisters," she said, her eyes wide, "I fear we've been going about this all wrong. Think about it. What Reeves and Gilli really need is a wife and mother."

"Someone to understand Gilli," Magnolia murmured, comprehension beginning to glow in her eyes, "and someone to lighten Reeves's heavy spirit."

"Someone like Anna Miranda!" Odelia chirped.

Hypatia smiled, praising God in her heart, for He always had more in mind for His children than they themselves sometimes dared to dream. And if in this case He didn't, well, it wouldn't hurt to pray about the matter, would it?

Chapter Three

Sitting at her usual table in the little coffee shop across from the BCBC campus, Anna huddled over her steaming mug and yawned, trying to shake the cobwebs from her mind. She'd worked late into the night, prompted by a phone call from her grandmother, who had only just learned from some committee member that Anna was handling the BCBC fund-raiser account. As usual, Tansy had displayed no faith whatsoever in Anna's abilities, lecturing her on the importance of the assignment and her responsibilities to her employer and the cause. Anna had hung up on her, not an uncommon occurrence, and set to work. Now she had two good reasons for wanting to do her best. To her surprise, the first appeared at her elbow.

"Hard night?"

She looked up at the handsome face of Reeves Leland, handsome but somewhat haggard despite being cleanly shaved. "I could ask the same of you."

"Or you could just ask me to sit down."

She looked around, saw that the other tables were full and nodded. He sprawled across the chair with a sigh, hanging an elbow on the edge of the tabletop.

"I haven't seen you in here before."

He slugged back coffee from the disposable cup in his hand, wincing at the heat. "I usually wait and get my caffeine at the office, but this morning I need a little extra fortification just to get there. Figured I might as well order a hot roll while I was at it." He glanced at the counter. "Does it usually take this long?"

"Mornings are busy," she said. "So why the extra fortification?"

He grimaced. "I worked all night, and Gilli was on a tear this morning." He shook his head and sucked up more brew.

"Well, that makes two of us," she said, "working late, that is." He lifted an eyebrow. "What? You don't think I ever put in long hours?"

"Did I say that?"

"You didn't have to." She cut her gaze away, muttering, "And here I thought you'd come to cry peace."

He straightened in his chair and set his cup on the table, folding his arms behind it. "I think that's a very good idea, actually." She shot him a startled, wary glance, and he lifted a hand in a gesture of openness. "It wasn't what I had in mind when I was looking around for an empty seat, but now that you mention it…" He rolled his shoulders beneath his overcoat. "I don't see why we should be enemies over stuff that happened ages ago."

Recalling some of that "stuff," Anna grinned. "That's very generous of you, Stick. You mean you forgive me for busting up your baseball bat?"

His forehead furrowed. "How did you do that? I've always wondered."

"Nothing to it. I just carried it down to the tracks and waited for a train to come by, then tossed the pieces back in your yard."

He shook his head, one corner of his mouth curling up. "Guess we should've let you play, huh? I almost did, but the other guys never would've let me forget it."

"I didn't think about that."

"Why am I not surprised?"

She stuck her tongue out at him, and he laughed, his eyes crinkling up around the edges. "There's that brat again."

It was perhaps the first time he'd ever actually laughed at her. Picking at her napkin, she tried not to read too much into it, but she couldn't help asking, "So, you ever going to forgive me for gluing your car keys to your locker door?"

"Not a chance." He wagged a finger at her. "Do you have any idea what that cost? I had to replace the ignition module to get a working key for the car, not to mention the locker door."

She jerked up onto the edge of her seat. "They made you replace the locker door?"

He suddenly seemed uncomfortable. "They didn't *make me* exactly."

"But you did it anyway," she surmised, shocked. "You must have because they didn't make me do it." She'd sat in two weeks of detention, but nothing had been said about financial reparation.

For several seconds Reeves sat very still. Then he tilted his head slightly and confessed, "It wouldn't have hurt me to give you a ride that day. I never figured you'd walk all the way to school in the rain. I just thought your grandmother would take you."

"She wasn't there that morning," Anna told him, "one of her committee meetings or something." He closed his eyes and shook his head. She instantly took pity on him, saying, "Look, it's not your fault. I could have called someone else, but after you said no, I was so mad I just struck out on foot. Later, when you dropped your keys, well, I couldn't resist."

He shook his head, saying softly, "Kids do stupid things."

"Yeah, well, I think I probably did more than my fair share."

He looked up from beneath the crag of his brow. "I think you probably did, too."

She tried for outrage but wound up spluttering laughter. He joined in, and it was perhaps the first moment of real camaraderie they'd ever shared.

"So," she asked, making small talk, "what were you up all night working on?"

"Aw, we've got this big negotiation with a new fuel provider. I was putting together the figures, trying to estimate their costs and our—" He broke off suddenly, his eyes going wide. "The figures!" He smacked himself in the forehead with the heel of his palm. "They're in my laptop, which I left at the house! Oh, man." On his feet before he'd finished speaking, he started for the door.

"What about your roll?"

"Uh, you eat it. I've gotta run. Sorry. I'll, uh, be seeing you."

"Right. Later. Maybe," she said, her voice waning as he rushed out the door.

After a moment she turned back to contemplate the coffee in her mug, wondering what had just happened. Had she and Reeves Leland actually taken a step toward putting the past behind them? If so, then what else might be possible?

She was afraid even to contemplate the answer to that question.

Irritated, Reeves quietly let himself into the house via the front entry hall. He never left his laptop behind, but he'd just been so frazzled this morning. If only Gilli hadn't awakened in the same petulant mood that she'd gone to sleep in, he might not have forgotten the thing. Sneaking about made him cringe, but he took care to walk softly just the same. The last thing he wanted was for Gilli to see him and pitch another fit for him to stay home—as if he could! He had almost passed by the open door of the front parlor when the sound of his own name brought him to an abrupt halt.

"Reeves is perfect!"

Well, that was nice to hear, but what followed knocked the breath out of him.

"He's perfect for Anna Miranda! I can't believe I didn't think of this earlier."

"Now, Tansy," Aunt Hypatia said, an edge to her voice that none of her nephews or nieces would dare to ignore, "don't get carried away. It's just a thought, a matter for prayer. Odelia was simply mentioning a possibility in passing, one she would have done better to keep to herself, obviously."

"There must be something I can do," Tansy went on, ignoring Hypatia. "Anna never has more than a few dates with a fellow. If I leave it to her, she'll never marry."

Reeves had his doubts about that. Plenty of men were bound to be interested in a woman as attractive and clever as Anna Miranda. Just not him. True, he'd seen a different side of her this morning, a compelling side, but she had demonstrated that the brat was ready and willing to reemerge at a moment's notice, and he had no intention of dealing with that. Best to nip the idiotic notion in the bud right now. Sucking in a deep breath, he strode through the doorway.

Hypatia winced as Odelia exclaimed with innocent delight. "Reeves! We were just talking about you." Red enamel hoops a good two inches wide dangled from her earlobes.

"So I heard."

Mags asked warily, "Shouldn't you be at work?"

Reeves gave her a frown. "Yes, and I would be if I hadn't left my laptop in my room." He settled a narrow look on Tansy Burdett, adding, "Fortunately."

"Reeves, dear," Hypatia began apologetically, "please don't think—"

"No, no," Tansy interrupted, getting to her feet. "*Do* think about it. You need a wife. My granddaughter needs a husband."

Reeling from that pronouncement, Reeves watched as she

drew herself up to her full height, which must have been all of five feet, including the tall thick heels of her brown pumps and the helmet-like perfection of her chin-length, pale yellow hair. Slight and angular, with sharp features and faded blue eyes, she wore a white cotton blouse and a straight skirt beneath a boxy jacket.

"And that's all there is to it?" he scoffed, incredulous.

Lifting her chin, Tansy met him eye to eye and proclaimed, "You're a good Christian man with a sound head on your shoulders, despite the mistake you made the first time around. Besides, Anna Miranda's always had a thing for you."

Now *that* was absurd. Anna Miranda had a thing for him, all right. He'd always been her favorite target, a butt for jokes, a subject for pranks, an object of ridicule.

"I have no intention of marrying again," Reeves said to Tansy, exasperated, "and certainly not to—" He couldn't even say it. Anna Miranda Burdett and *him?* Instead, he turned on his aunties, focusing on Hypatia. "Surely you do not believe that she…we…. Tell me you haven't been matchmaking."

"Now, Reeves," Hypatia said calmly, "it was nothing more than idle chatter. We merely agreed to pray about it, that's all."

"Pray as you like, Aunt Hypatia," he grit out, "but leave my private life to me!" He hadn't meant to raise his voice, but he had done just that, which was why he winced and said, "Sorry."

"No offense taken, dear," Hypatia remarked meekly. "It's just that we're so concerned for you and Gilli."

"She needs a mother, dear," Odelia put in.

"She *has* a mother," he snapped, knowing that in Marissa's case it was little more than a title, despite the allusions and veiled threats of late.

Marissa continued to complain of financial difficulty, and lately she'd started mentioning that she missed Gilli. For their daughter's sake, he wished that were so, but he knew better. Marissa had no more desire to see Gilli than she'd had to give birth to her. He regretted offering her joint custody now, but at the time he'd hoped she would actually use it to be part of their daughter's life, not browbeat him for money.

And they thought they could convince him to marry again!

All three of the aunties bowed their heads in contrition. Tansy merely flattened her mouth and tugged at the hem of her jacket, sharp chin aloft, before dropping back down into her chair with a huff.

Reeves pinched the bridge of his nose, eyes closed, and counted to ten before carefully saying, "Look, I appreciate your concern, but I don't want any more talk about matchmaking, not with Anna Miranda, not with anyone. Is that clear?" The aunts gave him nods and wan smiles. "Now, if you'll excuse me," he managed, "I have to get to the office." Turning on his heel, he swiftly left the room and headed for the stairs.

Behind him, he heard Odelia say, "Poor Reeves."

"No more matchmaking talk," Hypatia instructed quickly.

Poor Reeves. How pathetic. The thought of the aunties meddling in his life both shocked and hurt, but he knew that he really had no one to blame except himself. He had mucked it all up. Sighing, he hurried up the stairs, intent on getting that laptop and out of the house before anything else could happen to delay him.

But he could not get over the thought of Anna Miranda and him as a couple.

Wherever would the aunts get such a preposterous idea? Anna Miranda Burdett and him! He wondered how long it would be before he could get that ridiculous notion out of his head.

Anna's determination to show Reeves that his aunts were right to trust her with this project only grew after their meeting in the coffee shop. That resolve turned a couple days of work into four, but excitement gripped her as she waited at the sunny yellow, black-framed door at the front of the enormous house late that next Friday afternoon. Chester Worth, the Chatam's long-time driver and houseman, opened it for her.

"Miss Anna, come on in here out of the cold."

"Thank you, Chester." She held a soft spot for Chester, who had never in her memory referred to her as anything but Miss Anna. "I called ahead. The Chatams should be expecting me."

"They surely are. Miss Hypatia and Miss Odelia are in the parlor, and Miss Magnolia will join y'all shortly. I'll bring in the tea soon as she shows up."

Anna smiled. "I'll let the others know."

Chester went on his way, and Anna walked into the spacious, elegant front parlor. Odelia hopped up and hurried forward to hug her, chains of orange crystals hanging from her earlobes. She wore a long, multi-colored, gathered skirt with a melon pink blouse, wide black belt and purple vest. Hypatia, in contrast, looked the picture of prim wealth in a tailored, moss-green pantsuit and pearls. She, too, rose and came to meet Anna with a smile and handclasp.

They were still exchanging greetings when Mags trundled into the room, smelling of loam and flowers. She seemed to own only one dress, or else they all looked alike. This one she wore with a pair of brown slacks, a moth-eaten gray cardigan and red-rimmed black galoshes. Anna managed not to laugh. Mags beamed back at her and plopped down on the settee.

Anna quickly extracted three copies of four designs from her portfolio, passing them to the sisters. They were still exclaiming over her nature design when Chester arrived with the tea tray. A quarter-hour later, they sat balancing delicate, steaming Limoges teacups on matching saucers while Anna explained the second design to them. Odelia, predictably, gushed, but Mags screwed up her face at the ribbons and lace, while Hypatia made the sort of nice comments that one made when complimenting a beaming bride in a particularly heinous gown. She was obviously better pleased with the "biblical" design that followed.

Finally, Anna introduced the fourth rendering. "This," she said neutrally, "is something of a combination of the other three in what I like to think of as the definitive Chatam House spirit."

The effect was immediate, gasps, clattering of cups and saucers, oohs of pleasure.

"Anna Miranda," Hypatia exclaimed, holding out the sheet to gaze at it, "this is…"

"Gorgeous!" Odelia finished for her.

Mags actually sniffed. "Those are magnolias in the swag, aren't they?"

"Seemed apt," Anna told her with a fond, pleased smile.

Hypatia placed the sheet of paper reverently atop the piecrust tea table and folded her hands. "Well, I think it's obvious—"

Suddenly Odelia interjected herself. "Oh, but the romantic one is so…romantic."

Mags sat up straight. "What are you talking about?"

"Now, I know you prefer the nature one," Odelia cut in, "but this is an important decision. It needs time." Ophelia tapped the little watch pendant pinned to her blouse and waved obliquely toward the door.

Mags stared at her for a moment then her eyebrows shot up. "But he said—"

"Talk," Odelia interrupted hurriedly. "No more *talk.* E-except about the design."

Mags blinked at that then she cleared her throat. "Ah. Well, it's just that m-my idea is the best. Uh, the way Anna Miranda has designed it, that is."

"Now, sisters," Hypatia began sternly, but once more Odelia charged in.

"You don't agree that we should *talk* about the designs a little more?"

Hypatia seemed uncomfortable. She actually fidgeted, shifting her trim weight side to side. Anna sat fascinated, not at all certain what was going on but entranced by the sisterly byplay. She said not a word as Odelia and Magnolia entered into a spirited debate of their individual preferences.

Some minutes later, Chester entered to remove the tea tray. Bending over it, he looked straight at Odelia and announced, "Mr. Reeves is home."

With that, he straightened and exited the room. Odelia popped up and scuttled after him as far as the doorway. At the same time, footsteps could be heard in the back of the central hallway. Odelia produced a lace-edged hanky, which she began waving.

"Yoo-hoo! Reeves, dear! Can you help us please?"

Several heartbeats passed, during which the only sound was that of Hypatia softly moaning. Finally, Reeves said, "Of course."

Anna twisted in her chair and leaned over the arm to watch Odelia grasp his elbow and pull him bodily into the parlor.

"We just can't decide," she trilled, tugging him forward. "Anna Miranda's done such a marvelous job for us, but we just can't agree. Give us your opinion, won't you?"

She hauled him over to the table, where Magnolia laid out the four options for him. Reeves slid a hooded glance at Anna before quickly bending over the table. Anna held her breath. After a moment, he turned a look in her direction, surprised appreciation in his copper-brown eyes.

"These are quite good."

She managed a blasé nod and a dry, "Thanks."

He went back to the designs, tapping the fourth with the tip of one forefinger. "This one's the best."

Anna stifled a crow of delight.

"Well," Hypatia said, sounding relieved, "that's that."

Odelia jerked, all but physically throwing herself back into the fray. "Oh, but…what about the staff?"

"The staff?" Mags echoed.

"They ought to have a say in this. We'll be depending on them, after all, to keep everything running smoothly the night of the auction."

"Odelia," Hypatia said wearily, pressing her fingertips to her temples.

Undetered, Odelia began gathering up the designs. "I know, we'll take these back to the kitchen." She nudged her sisters to their feet. "We'll each make our case, and see what Chester, Hilda and Carol have to say. That seems fair, doesn't it?"

Hypatia sighed and sent an apologetic look to Reeves, who lifted a hand to the back of his neck. Absolutely no one, including Anna, was surprised when Odelia turned to him and instructed, "Now, Reeves, dear, you'll entertain Anna Miranda for us for a few minutes, won't you?" She began pushing and shooing her sisters from the room. "So rude to leave her sitting here on her own, you know."

Anna watched the whole thing in bemused fascination, especially the part where Odelia winked at Reeves then pinched her thumb and forefinger together and drew them across her lips in a zipping motion.

"Yeah, thanks for that," he said wryly.

Anna waited until their footsteps receded before favoring him with a direct look, her elbows braced against the arms of the chair. "What on earth is that about?"

"Don't ask," he grumbled, sliding his hands into the pockets of his slacks. "Just let this be a lesson to you. Be very, very exact when dealing with my aunts."

"They can be a little…scattered."

He snorted. "That's one word for it."

"Actually, I think they're very sweet."

"Well, of course, they're sweet!" he exclaimed. "That's half the problem."

"What problem?" she shot back, stung. "I wasn't aware there was a problem, unless having to give your opinion has strained your brain."

"Ha-ha. Very funny. I hope you didn't pull a muscle coming up with that one."

"Oh, for pity's sake!" Anna shot to her feet and side-stepped the table. Why did he have to be so difficult, anyway? She thought they'd gotten past this.

Just then, Anna caught a muffled roaring sound, followed swiftly by a shrill, elongated scream. The next instant, Gilli burst into the room, wailing like a police siren, and shot across the floor on, of all things, roller skates, the cheap plastic sort that strapped over the soles of the shoes. She headed straight for the antique Empire breakfront in the corner. Reeves leapt forward to snatch up a priceless Tiffany lamp, while Anna lunged with outstretched arms for Gilli.

The pair of them went down in a tangle of limbs. Fortunately, they missed the tall Federal table in the center of the floor and the enormous flower arrangement atop it. A small elbow landed in Anna's midsection, knocking the air out of her in a painful rush. For one long moment, all was silent and still. Then a sigh gusted forth, and Reeve's handsome head, paired up nicely with a stained glass lampshade, appeared above her.

"And so," he muttered, "goes my life."

Anna laughed. The look on his face, the droll tone of his voice, the memory of Gilli's flailing arms as she flew across the floor, even the collision that had Anna on her back—again—gazing up at his resigned, hangdog expression, it all suddenly seemed like something out of an old slapstick comedy. Oh, how little he appreciated that, but his frowns merely made her laugh that much harder. It had been a long time since she'd had this much fun. Too long. She pushed up onto her elbows, Gilli sprawled all over her, and as was too often the case, said the first thing that came to mind.

"You know something, Stick? I've missed you."

He couldn't have looked more appalled if she'd decorated him with her lunch, but that didn't change a thing. She had missed him. She had missed him every single day since he'd graduated from high school, and some part of her always would.

She had missed him.

The idea warmed, shocked and alarmed Reeves all at the same time. He recognized the glow in the corner of his heart with disgust. Was he so desperate to be loved that even an offhanded quip from a girl who had all but tortured him could produce such a reaction? Or was it Tansy and the aunties who had put that into his mind?

Groaning, he decided that God must be punishing him. That had to be the case. Yet, had Solomon not written that the Lord disciplines those He loves?

But does it have to be her, Lord? he asked in silent prayer. *Isn't Gilli enough?*

Horrified that he'd thought of his own child as punishment, Reeves reached down a hand to help as Gilli began struggling up onto her knees. It was Anna Miranda's hand that found his, however, and with his other still clutching the Tiffany lamp, he had little choice but to haul her up. She came to her feet with a little hop and a cheeky smile. Gilli collapsed upon the hardwood floor and began to wail as if she'd broken all four limbs.

Tamping down his impatience with such melodrama, Reeves turned to set aside the lamp so he could help his daughter up, but when he turned back, she was already on her feet, thanks to Anna Miranda. Gilli abruptly yanked away from her, and threw herself at Reeves with a cry of outrage, her skates slipping and sliding as she clamped her arms around his thighs. Reeves sent an embarrassed look at Anna Miranda before grasping Gilli by the shoulders and holding her far enough away that he could look down into her face. He saw more petulance there than pain or fear.

"Cut it out," he ordered over the din of phony sobs.

"I fell down!" she defended hotly.

The last tenuous thread of Reeves's patience snapped. "I said to cut it out!" he roared. As he rarely raised his voice to her, Gilli was shocked into frozen silence.

Not so Anna Miranda, who brought her hands to her slender hips and snapped, "*You* cut it out. It's all your own fault, you know."

Exasperated, Reeves glared at her. "*My* fault? I didn't come flying in here on skates."

"No, but you might have taught her to skate properly before this," Anna reasoned.

Gilli immediately seized on that notion. "Yes, Daddy! Teach me! Please, please!"

He ignored her, focusing on the one who'd opened this can of worms. "And how am I supposed to do that?" he demanded. "Look at her. She's not old enough for that."

"I am!" Gilli insisted, her tears suddenly dried.

"Of course she is," Anna Miranda agreed, folding her arms.

"I think I know my daughter better than you do, thank you very much. Besides, I don't even own a pair of skates myself, let alone all the necessary safety equipment for the two of us."

"So get some," Anna Miranda retorted.

"I got skates!" Gilli interjected desperately. "Real skates. My mama brought them at Christmas."

"Sent them," Reeves corrected distractedly. "She *sent* you a pair of roller skates, but they're too big for you." Gilli had waited with breathless anticipation for her mother to arrive for Christmas as Marissa had promised during her one visit some six months ago, but all that had arrived was a crumpled card and a pair of roller skates with hard pink-and-purple plastic boots two sizes too large.

"They're not too big!" Gilli insisted. "And I'm old. I am!"

Reeves pinched the bridge of his nose. "Gilli, I'm not going to argue about this. All I need is you flailing around here on skates. You'll break a leg. Or worse."

"All the more reason to teach her," Anna Miranda insisted.

It was the last straw for Reeves. Lifting Gilli by her upper arms, he sat her in a nearby Victorian lyre-back chair and began stripping off the cheap demi-skates, which consisted of nothing more than rollers attached to a platform that belted to shoes with fasteners. He'd thought to placate her with them when she'd discovered that she couldn't wear the "real" skates that her mother had sent, but he hadn't realized she could get the demi ones on by herself, which was why he hadn't refused when she'd insisted on bringing both pairs with her to Chatam House.

"When you become a parent," he told Anna Miranda coldly, "maybe your opinion will matter."

"You know what your problem is, Stick?" she shot back. "Your problem is that you were never a child."

Straightening, he whirled. "That's rich coming from someone who has obviously never grown up!"

"And who never wants to, if growing up means achieving pure stupidity."

"Stupid would be teaching my daughter to do something so dangerous as skating!"

"As opposed to letting her teach herself, I suppose."

"As opposed to dropping these in the nearest trash can!" he yelled, holding up the skates by their plastic straps.

Gilli threw herself off the chair and pelted from the room, yowling her outrage at the top of her lungs. Reeves sighed, slumping dejectedly. Wow, he'd handled that well. Once more, he'd let the brat get to him, and he didn't mean his daughter. What was it about Anna Miranda Burdett that turned him into a crude adolescent? And why could he never hit the right note with his daughter?

Father, forgive me, he prayed, squeezing his eyes shut. *I fail at every turn, and I'm as tired of me as You must be. In the name of Christ Jesus, please help me do better!*

He sucked in a deep breath and grated out an apology. "I didn't mean to shout."

"Well, you sure do plenty of it" was Anna Miranda's droll reply. She glared at him from behind folded arms.

Suddenly, Reeves craved a run with every fiber of his being. Maybe some exercise and a long, private talk with God would give him the serenity and clarity to deal with this latest insanity. Loosening his tie, he said to Anna Miranda in what he felt was a very reasonable tone, "Please tell my aunts that I've gone for a run before dinner."

Some seconds ticked by before she reluctantly nodded. Reeves headed for his room and the numb exhaustion of a hard run in the February cold, more heartsick than angry now and helpless to do a thing about any of it.

Intellectually, he knew that Gilli's behavior had to do with her mother's abandonment. Marissa hadn't even said goodbye to Gilli before she'd slammed out of the house and run down the drive to jump onto the back of her boyfriend's motorcycle, which made her recent communication all the more absurd. Marissa had been a pitiful mother, but Gilli couldn't know that. All she knew was that her mother had walked out, and she seemed to blame him. It hurt far more than he would ever let on. In fact, nothing in his life had ever made Reeves feel like such a failure as Gilli's resentment of him, which was undoubtedly why he had been so rude to Anna Miranda just now. For some reason, it embarrassed him to have her know in how little regard his own daughter held him.

That, of course, was no excuse. As he changed into his jogging outfit, he apologized to God once again for his behavior and attitude. He would do better, he vowed. He would do better with Gilli and, God help him, with Anna Miranda, too. Somehow.

Chapter Four

It seemed to Anna that Reeves needed to be taught a lesson. He needed to learn that his daughter could, indeed, learn to skate—and behave—given enough time, attention, patience and praise. Surely, once she showed up with all the requisite gear, he'd have to let her try; otherwise, Gilli would never forgive him. Maybe he wouldn't be happy about it, but, oh, well. Anna would not even consider that he might be right about Gilli being too young. She'd get Gilli rolling if it killed her. Then let the big goof tell her what an immature idiot she was.

Reeves wasn't the only reason Anna wanted to do this, though. She felt for Gilli, recognized the yawning, unknowing need in her. What that poor kid really wanted was attention and reassurance, not constant criticism and impatient, domineering control.

The Chatam triplets returned to declare the "classic Chatam House" motif their choice. They seemed deflated at finding her alone in the parlor, but Anna merely smiled, delivered Reeves's message and promised to return tomorrow with samples of the motif printed on various papers.

The next day was Saturday and Valentine's Day, to boot,

but Anna saw no reason to delay, especially considering what she had in mind for Gilli. She swung by the shop to pick up sample papers, then as soon as she got home pulled down her old in-line skates from the top shelf of her bedroom closet. Next, she went to work on the mock-ups. Once her personal printer had spit out those, Anna set about designing a pair of hand-drawn Valentines, one for the triplets, using the Chatam House theme, to thank them for their business and unfailing kindness, and a glittery one for Gilli, featuring a curly-haired little girl pirouetting on roller skates while wearing a pink tutu, muffler and mittens.

After a quick dinner, Anna made a run to the local discount store and bought protective gear for Gilli, stuffing it into a big, pink paper bag with red tissue paper, confident that she would have put Reeves Leland firmly in his place by noon the next day. As she slipped into bed that night, she told herself that, for once, Valentine's Day promised to be sweet, indeed.

Hypatia answered the front door at Chatam House the next morning. Dressed in a lovely soldier blue, cowl-neck knit sheath and buckled pumps dyed to match, with pearls at her throat and her silver hair twisted into its usual smooth chignon at her nape, she looked fit to meet the Queen of England over tea; her smile could not have been more gracious if she had been.

"Good morning, dear," she all but sang. The gray morning seemed to brighten.

"Good morning!"

"Come in, please." Anna stepped into the spacious entry hall and set aside her portfolio and the gift bag to shrug out of her coat while Hypatia continued to speak. "What is that you have there, dear?"

Anna turned to smile over one shoulder. "Just a little something for a little someone. And the paper samples, of course."

"Of course. How very prompt you are, and how kind of you to think of Gilli. It's very timely. She's in a bit of a snit because her father had to go in to work this morning."

Anna's spirits dimmed. She had been strangely looking forward to butting heads with Reeves again. This way was probably better, though.

"Maybe I can brighten Gilli's mood a bit," Anna said. "We had a little, er, skating altercation yesterday, and I thought I might give her a lesson. My gear's in the car."

"I'm sure she'll be delighted. We're still nursing our morning tea out in the sunroom. Won't you join us?"

"Yes, thank you."

Anna took up her leather portfolio and the gift bag to follow along behind Hypatia. Reeves would undoubtedly disapprove of her plans for Gilli. They might even argue about it after the fact. The possibility made Anna smile. She had forgotten what fun it was to argue with Reeves. His quick wit easily matched hers, and she found his innate sense of outrage deliciously ridiculous. She couldn't help feeling disappointed that she wouldn't see him this morning. The sunroom lifted her spirits significantly, however.

Two glass walls, numerous plants and groupings of comfortable bamboo furnishings upholstered in colorful fabric printed with oversized flowers gave the space an airy, tropical feel that bravely defied the gray Texas winter. Anna found the other two sisters lounging on matched chaises. A small table between them held teacups and saucers. Magnolia, she noted, wore her usual garb, while Odelia's red plaid jumper and yellow silk blouse warred violently with the upholstery upon which she reclined. The red enamel hearts clipped to her earlobes were the size of drink coasters. It was Gilli, however, who drew Anna's interest. Wearing jeans and a purple turtleneck, she sprawled half on, half off a deeply padded chair, her bottom lip sticking out in a pout.

"Looks like someone woke up on the wrong side of the

bed this morning," Anna remarked lightly, sinking down onto the plush chair that Hypatia indicated with a wave.

Magnolia sighed. "Reeves had to go in to work today. He's having some issues with an important negotiation."

"It's really not his fault," Odelia put in, glancing at Gilli, who made a rude sound and curled into a ball on the seat of the chair, covering her head with her arms.

Anna smiled to herself and placed the paper bag on the floor nearby. "What a shame," she said with a sigh. "I guess that means Gilli won't be interested in what I've brought her." Anna pulled the two handcrafted Valentine cards from her portfolio.

Gilli's arms relaxed, and her little chin with its tiny cleft lifted as she attempted to peer in Anna's direction without being too obvious about it. Anna passed one of the cards to Hypatia, saying, "This is for the three of you. Happy Valentine's Day."

Odelia clapped her hands as Hypatia extracted the card from its envelope.

"How lovely. Thank you, dear," Hypatia said, showing the front of the card to her sisters. She quickly read the sentiment penned inside and passed the card to Magnolia.

Magnolia passed the card to Odelia, smiling at Anna. "You do such good work, Anna Miranda, but what's in the bag, dear?"

"Oh," Anna said, "that goes with this second card, the one I'd hoped to give to a certain little girl."

Gilli sat up, her curiosity getting the better of her. "I'm a little girl," she said.

Anna bit back a chuckle. "So you are. The very little girl I had in mind, actually."

Gilli slid off her chair and went straight to the bag, but Hypatia forestalled her. "Card first, Gilli."

The girl paused, eyes wide. Smoothly, Anna offered the card to Gilli. "Happy Valentine's Day, sweetie."

Gilli's brow puckered. "What's Balertine?"

"It's a day for sweethearts," Odelia supplied, smiling beatifically, "when people who love each other exchange gifts."

Gilli stared at Anna, speculation lighting her copper-brown eyes. They were so like Reeves's that Anna's heart flipped over inside her chest. Gilli's gaze switched to the envelope. Anna carefully removed the card and held it out. Gilli pounced.

"Pretty!"

"Let us see," Odelia urged. Gilli ran to her great aunt, trailing glitter. Odelia gushed over the card, opening it and reading the sentiment inside. "Happy Valentine's Day to a roller-skating ballerina."

Gilli tilted her head, caramel-colored curls bouncing. "What's balaringa?"

Odelia tapped the drawing on the front of the card. "This is a ballerina. See her pretty dress?"

Gasping, Gilli ran to the bag. "Is it balaringa dress?"

"Nope," Anna replied as Gilli pulled the helmet from the bag. "It's what you need to learn to skate."

The girl instantly deflated, dropping the helmet and slumping her shoulders. "Daddy won't teach me."

"I will," Anna told her, reaching into the bag to remove the knee and elbow pads.

Gilli gasped and immediately turned pleading eyes on Hypatia, wheedling, "Can I? Pleeease, pleeeease? I'm old to skate."

Anna said nothing. Was it her fault if Reeves hadn't made his opinion on the matter clear to his aunts?

Hypatia exchanged glances with her sisters before saying, "I think some exercise would do you a world of good, Gilli. Thank you, Anna. Gilli, run upstairs to get your skates."

Gilli began to bounce up and down. "Skates! Skates! Skates!"

"I'll go with her," Odelia volunteered, swinging her legs off the chaise.

"And I'll get her coat from the cloakroom," Magnolia added.

"Bring extra pairs of thick socks, too," Anna said to Odelia, who had risen and taken Gilli by the hand. "The skates may be a little large for her."

"The extra socks will keep her warm," Hypatia noted.

"Skates! Skates! Skates!" Gilli chanted, hopping along beside Odelia as the older woman led her from the room, Magnolia on their heels.

"How thoughtful you are, Anna Miranda," Hypatia said with a gentle smile.

Anna shrugged and confessed, "I have an ulterior motive. I think Reeves needs to pay his daughter more attention, and I hope this shows him that she's old enough to reason with and not just scold."

Hypatia's smile widened. "You are answered prayer, my dear."

Taken aback by that, Anna passed the older woman her portfolio, babbling, "The…the samples…for you to look at."

"Ah," Hypatia purred, drawing the portfolio into her lap. "We'll talk again later."

Nodding, Anna shoved the pads and helmet back into the bag, then quickly excused herself and escaped to fetch her gear from the car. She left the bag at the foot of the stairs and returned moments later to find an excited Gilli with her helmet on backward, trying to tear her pads from their packaging. While Odelia clucked and Magnolia held Gilli's coat, Anna laughed to see Gilli so excited. She sat down on the stairs to help the girl properly don her new safety gear then put on her own before working the extra socks onto Gilli's feet.

"We'll put on our skates outside," she instructed.

"How come?"

"So we don't damage the floors or break any of your aunts' valuable antiques."

Gilli blinked at her then quickly gathered up her hard plastic skates, hugging them to her chest. Anna slung her own over one shoulder by the carry strap, while Odelia and Magnolia together managed to get Gilli into her coat.

With Gilli's great-aunts waving fondly, Anna ushered the girl out of the house and across the porch to the brick steps. It took several minutes to get skates on both of them. Anna donned her own first, and then buckled Gilli tightly into the pink-and-purple skates. They were a bit large as well as a little too tall, but they would do.

"Okey-doke, let's get out to the sidewalk."

That proved a major undertaking. Gilli literally threw herself toward the street, only to wind up sprawled facedown on the gravel drive. Though she wailed for a minute, she wasn't hurt. The gravel was very deep and served to cushion Gilli's fall; it also provided a perfect base for Gilli to learn to stand and walk in her skates. By the time they'd made their way down the drive to the edge of the property, Anna had almost convinced herself that she actually could accomplish her goal and teach Gilli to skate. Sort of. She hoped.

They reached the massive wrought-iron gate, which stood open, and used it to work their way past the grate between drive and street to the sidewalk beyond. A harrowing half hour followed, during which they both took several spills. Thankfully, neither suffered more than bruises, and gradually Anna found herself merely tense rather than terrified. Then, suddenly, everything seemed to click and Gilli was skating, or waddling on wheels, anyway. Gilli couldn't have been more thrilled.

Relieved, Anna's fatigue disappeared, and she began to instruct Gilli on technique, confident of success. She forgot all about tweaking Reeves and got swept up, instead, in the pride and joy on Gilli's sweet little face. They were both exhausted but laughing as they skated slowly, hand in hand and noses rosy, back toward the estate gate over an hour later.

They had almost reached it when a late model, silver, domestic sedan turned into the drive and stopped. The driver's door opened, and Reeves Leland got out, staring at them over the top of the car.

"Daddy!" Gilli called, waving. "Look! Look!"

Anna held her breath, suddenly wishing she'd gone about this whole thing differently. Why hadn't she realized that she might be overstepping? Gilli was his daughter; he had authority over her, not his aunts. He might be not just irritated but very angry with Anna. That did not seem like such a fun thing all of a sudden.

"I'm skating!" Gilli cried needlessly.

"So you are," Reeves said after a moment, and to Anna's everlasting relief, he smiled. His gaze shifted to Anna then, and the smile froze, looking a tad strained around the edges.

For the first time, no quip sprang to her tongue, no goading put-down, no clever crack or blistering boast. Instead, Anna drew Gilli to a halt at the edge of the drive and smiled tentatively, aware that Gilli babbled at her side about the morning's adventure. Reeves switched his attention back to his daughter, smiling down at her and nodding.

Finally, Gilli drew breath enough for Reeves to speak. "I guess you've grown into those skates, after all."

"They're actually a little large still," Anna confessed. "She's got on extra socks."

A shaft of sunlight broke through the clouds just then, lighting his face so that his eyes glinted like new pennies. "Guess it's a good thing it's winter."

"True." An awkward silence followed, and Anna felt a great urge to fill it. "Maybe by summer she'll truly have grown into them."

"Maybe," he said, looking down at Gilli. "If you'd like to take off your skates you can ride up to the house with me."

Gilli dropped Anna's hand and plopped down onto the cold sidewalk. Reeves came around to crouch beside her and help her remove the skates. He tapped a knuckle against her pink-and-purple helmet, asking, "Where did you get this?"

Gilli tilted her head back, looking up at Anna. "She got it."

Reeves looked up at Anna, his forearms balanced atop his knees. "That was very nice of her."

Anna muttered that it was nothing. She had never felt so off-kilter in her life. It was weird. This was not what she expected of Reeves. He was actually being nice to her.

He rose to open the back door of the car and drop the skates onto the floorboard while Gilli scrambled inside. Reeves got her into her safety seat, closed the door and turned to Anna. "How about you?"

"Huh?" The question made no sense to Anna, so she stood there gaping at him like a landed fish.

"Want a ride?"

"Oh! No, I'll just—" She almost bit her tongue off, realizing only belatedly what she'd said. Why had she refused a ride up to the house? Tired and beginning to feel chilled, she dreaded that deep gravel, but it was as if her brain had gone into hibernation. Before she could bully it to full wakefulness, Reeves got in behind the steering wheel.

An instant later, the car engine started. She watched the car move up the long drive and sighed before beginning the slog up to the house.

Things weren't turning out quite as she'd planned for some reason, but what could she do except trudge forward?

Gilli chattered happily all the way up the drive, something about ballerinas, as far as Reeves could tell. She casually mentioned falling down, as if it was no big deal, and actually laughed about "bonking" her head and how much she liked her helmet. Reeves marveled that this was the same kid who howled like she was being beaten with a whip if he so much as shook a finger in her face, not that he'd ever laid a hand on her in anger. His stepmother, Layla, often counseled him to spank Gilli, but he'd noticed that Layla never followed her own advice with his baby sister Myra, though in fairness Myra did tend to behave better than Gilli. Reeves knew instinctively that was his fault; he just didn't know what to do about it.

"And now I can skate!" Gilli announced, pride in every syllable. "But not in the house," she went on, barely drawing breath. "No, no, not in the house, because of the val'ble antikies."

"Antiques," Reeves corrected with a smile.

"What's antiks?"

"Furniture and things like that. Very old furniture and things. The aunties' house is full of them."

"If they're old, how come they don't throw them away," she wanted to know, "like you threw away my shirt?"

"Because, unlike old shirts, antiques are very rare. That means they cost a lot of money. That's why we have to be very careful with the aunties' things."

"Oh." She sounded surprised but also informed, as if she'd just made a discovery.

Reeves shook his head, wondering why he hadn't thought to explain that to her before. Anna Miranda obviously had, at least to a point. He glanced into the side mirror, watching Anna Miranda struggle up the graveled drive.

He hadn't been able to believe his eyes when he'd first seen Gilli and Anna Miranda skating toward him, holding hands. At first, he'd been angry enough to spit. Then, once he'd accepted the fact that Gilli had obviously learned to skate, he'd felt a flash of resentment because Anna Know-It-All Miranda had been right. Remembering his promise to God the evening before, he'd said a quick prayer and tried to analyze the situation clearly.

What he had seen after that was the triumphant smile on his daughter's face and, to his surprise, the wary expression on Anna Miranda's. He'd expected her to be smug, self-satisfied, perhaps even disdainful, but she had looked genuinely guarded, almost worried. With good reason. He hadn't exactly given her the benefit of the doubt since they'd become reacquainted. Just the opposite, in fact.

From the beginning, he had assumed that she was up to no good, entertaining herself at his expense. Yet, there sat Gilli in safety gear that perfectly matched her skates, beaming and chattering like the happiest of little girls. He had to admit that, whatever Anna Miranda's intentions, she had made his little girl very happy today.

It stung that he hadn't been the one to do that for his daughter. It even stung a bit than Anna Miranda had refused to ride up to the house with him, but he pushed that aside, determined to concentrate on the good she had done for Gilli. And him. His daughter obviously could respond to instruction if properly given.

He brought the sedan to a halt behind Anna Miranda's battered coupe, noting that she'd pasted a bumper sticker that said "Imagine Art" over a scratch on the trunk lid and covered a hole in her taillight with red plastic tape. He wondered if she couldn't afford better. The idea surprised him, for the Burdetts, while not in the same league as the Chatams, were known to be well-off.

After climbing out of the car, he went for Gilli. She reached up, and because she was in her stocking feet, he pulled her into his arms and carried her toward the steps. It occurred to him that he hadn't actually held her in a long time, and he was surprised by how much she had grown, how much she had changed. Her little muscles felt strong and lean. She wasn't a baby anymore, and the realization clutched at his heart.

"Want to see my balaringa?" she asked hopefully.

"I think you mean ballerina, yes?"

Gilli nodded eagerly. "Her dress is so pretty. It sparkles, too. Wanna see?"

"Okay. Where is it?"

"Auntie 'Patia gots it, and she got one, too, but it is the house on it, and no sparkles." She slashed a hand downward, emphasizing the sad lack of sparkles.

"Ah."

He had no idea what she was talking about, not even when she said, "Anna did it."

"Is that so?"

Gilli nodded enthusiastically. Reeves glanced down the drive. Anna Miranda was finally drawing near, huffing and puffing with the effort. He felt Gilli's arm slip around his neck, and a love so strong and poignant seized him that it constricted his throat. He looked at her and saw the undiluted pride and joy in her eyes. It broke open something inside his chest, something cold and hard that he hadn't even known existed. It hurt, ached, but he felt an odd sense of relief, too, as if a boil had been lanced.

Anna Miranda drew up at last, leaning against the rear fender of his car. Reeves hefted Gilli a little higher against his chest and asked her, "Have you thanked Anna Miranda for your new things and teaching you to skate?"

Gilli leaned toward Anna Miranda and shouted, "Thank you!" Apparently in her world volume added weight to gratitude.

Before Reeves could scold her, Anna Miranda laughed and shouted back. "You're welcome!"

Gilli giggled behind her hands. For several seconds he could do nothing but revel in his daughter's sweet laughter, glad that he hadn't prevented it with his scolding. Finally, he turned and carried her up the steps.

"Go tell the aunties how well you're skating now," Reeves instructed, opening the front door and setting her on her feet in the foyer. "I'll bring your skates in after I speak with Anna Miranda."

Gilli waved at Anna Miranda and ran down the hallway, yelling, "I can skate! For real! I can skate!"

Reeves pulled the door closed and turned to address Anna Miranda. He didn't quite know how to behave with her. They'd been at loggerheads for so long, despite the years without contact. Those few minutes in the coffee shop were his only frame of reference for dealing with her on a normal basis. She lifted her helmet off her head, holding it against her hip with one hand while ruffling her hair with the other. She looked tired and mussed and perfectly adorable.

Adorable?

Shaking his head, Reeves descended the shallow steps and simply said, "Thanks."

Her delicate brows rose, her light, pure blue eyes widening. A smile tugged at her lips. "And?"

Of course, she would have her pound of flesh. Ah, well, in this case she deserved it. "And," he said slowly, "you were right."

Anna laid her head back against the roof of his car, her gaze moving back and forth. "Excuse me while I check to see if the sky is falling."

He fought a sudden smile. "Very funny. But, really, you shouldn't have done it."

Her gaze sharpened, instantly defensive. "Your aunts gave me permission."

"I didn't mean *that.*"

"Well, what did you mean, then?" she snapped. "That I'm not a capable teacher? I think events prove otherwise."

Reeves sucked in air and counted to ten. He would not, would *not,* let her spike his temper. Again. "I meant that you shouldn't have spent your money on Gilli. I'll reimburse you the cost of the helmet and pads."

"No, you won't." She pushed away from the car and made her way to the steps, where she sat and began removing her skates.

Reeves swallowed the argument that wanted to batter its way out of his mouth and changed the subject, asking,

"What's this about a ballerina? And something about the house?"

Anna Miranda looked up at him, smiling crookedly. "I made Valentine cards for Gilli and your aunts last night."

Reeves's mouth dropped open an instant before he pressed both palms to his temples. "This is the fourteenth! It's Valentine's Day!" And he had nothing for his daughter or aunts. Anna dropped one brow. Her expression seemed to say that he was the biggest idiot in creation. He couldn't disagree. "Oh, man. I completely forgot! There's this negotiation at work, and my house is all torn apart, and..."

Why even bother explaining? She'd still think he was an abysmal failure as a father and nephew, and she would be right. His aunts and daughter didn't have to know that he'd forgotten about them, though. He shoved aside his overcoat and dug his hand into the pockets of his pants for his keys.

"I—I have to go. J-just say I'll be back in a minute, would you? Please, Anna Miranda."

"Okay," she said, and he pivoted to leave, but then she added, "provided..."

Reeves froze then slowly turned back. "Provided what?" he asked sharply.

She looked him square in the eye. "Provided you stop calling me Anna Miranda."

Of all the things she could have said, that was the last one he might have expected. "What else would I call you?"

"Anna!" she exclaimed, as if it ought to somehow be obvious. "Just Anna. It is my first name, you know."

"B-but," he sputtered, "you've always been—"

"Anna Miranda was a child," she interrupted hotly. "Anna is an adult. Surely you've noticed that I am an adult."

Oh, he had noticed, all right. He was noticing at that very moment, and it made him want to run fast in the opposite direction. But he owed her. Heaven help him, he owed Anna Mir—uh, Anna Burdett.

"I, um, won't be long," he said, easing back a step. "Anna."

Going back to her skates, she him cut a sly look from the corners of her eyes. "Should I tell Gilli that you'll have a surprise for her?"

"Um, okay." Except… Surprise? He'd thought a card, something appropriately girlie. That suddenly seemed laughably inadequate now. He had the feeling that Anna Mir—make that just plain Anna—would have a suggestion. Not quite believing that he was doing this, he asked, "What sort of surprise would you recommend?"

A smile came and went on her face. "There's a reason chocolate is a traditional Valentine's Day gift. Females love it, females of every age."

Was that a hint? he wondered. Surely not, but… "Will you be here when I get back?"

"Maybe. I have some stuff to go over with your aunts."

"I won't be long," Reeves promised again, hurrying around to drop down behind the steering wheel of his sedan.

He probably ought to have his head examined for what he was about to do, but he couldn't see any other option. He couldn't very well give his aunts and Gilli gifts in front of Anna Miranda. Rather, *Anna.* Besides, he owed her for teaching Gilli to skate. He would just have to pick up something for *Anna,* too. The idea made him distinctly nervous, but then he thought of a way to blunt the impact, so to speak. He'd also buy small gifts for the household staff. It was only fair. Hilda, Carol and Chester looked after Gilli as much as his aunts did, and they took care of him, too. Yes, he definitely ought to demonstrate his gratitude to the staff of Chatam House.

"Thank You for the reminder, Lord, and thank You again for the sanctuary of Chatam House," he whispered as he started the car and made the loop in the driveway that would take him back to the street. "I'm trying to take advantage of this opportunity that You've given me to do better with my daughter." He drew a deep breath before adding, "And thank You for Anna. I'm trying to do better with her, too."

Who knew? They might even wind up friends.

Now, wouldn't that be a kick in the head?

Chapter Five

"How wonderful," Hypatia said in reply to Gilli's exuberant account of her adventure in skating.

Gilli's head bobbed like a bouncing rubber ball, and all the while she chattered. "They aren't too big for extra socks. My nose got cold, but not my toes, and not my hands and not my head. And it didn't even hurt when I fell down." She glanced around, then asked, "Where's Daddy?"

"He'll be in soon," Anna told her, "with a surprise."

Gilli gasped.

"You must be hungry after all that exercise," Magnolia said, getting to her feet. "Hilda ought to have something special to eat in the kitchen."

"Excellent," Hypatia said as Magnolia trundled off. "Now about the samples…"

Gilli got up to hang over the arm of Anna's chair, but she quickly grew tired of the conversation and began to whine until Magnolia came in bearing a tray crowded with the paraphernalia of a proper tea, including a platter of heart-shaped cookies with red icing. Moments later, when Reeves came in, a big bag in one hand and Gilli's skates in the other, Gilli was sitting on the floor at the end of the coffee table, drinking milk from a cup with a chip on the bottom rim and munching on cookies. Hypatia rescued the teacup when Gilli leaped up and literally threw herself at her father.

"Now, now," Reeves admonished mildly, working his way around the table. "Patience." He sat on the floor with Gilli. Mags jumped up to go for another cup, but he forestalled her. "Wait! I have something for you to take to the kitchen with you."

"What is it? What is it?" Gilli screeched, bouncing on her knees.

He held her off with one hand while he delved into the bag with the other, pulling out at least a half-dozen envelopes and a like number of small heart-shaped candy boxes, which he placed on the top of the coffee table. Gilli squealed with delight as he matched the cards to the boxes and passed them out.

"This is for you," he said, handing his daughter the pink box and envelope. While she shredded the envelope to get at the card inside, he simultaneously placed a red box and white envelope in Hypatia's lap and a flowered box and purple envelope in Odelia's.

"My favorite!" Odelia exclaimed, clutching the box of chocolate-covered cherries.

"And mine," Hypatia said, over the box of solid chocolates in her lap.

Magnolia got chocolate-covered pecan pralines, to her laughing delight, and a bright green envelope. He handed over two more cards and boxes, one of the latter larger than the other.

"These are for Carol and Hilda and Chester," Reeves told. "I didn't think I ought to buy Chester his own box. What do you think?"

"I'd say not," Mags told him, pointing to the white satin box and pale blue envelope left on the table, "but then who is that for?"

Anna's heart sped up when Reeves's gaze met hers. *For me?* she thought, swallowing a gasp.

"To thank you," he said, as if he'd read her mind.

Odelia squeaked like a mouse. Magnolia shot her sister an oddly triumphant glance as she turned away, laden with goodies for the kitchen. It was Hypatia's calm, warm smile that helped Anna reach forward with trembling fingers to gather in the box of assorted chocolates and the card.

"H-happy Valentine's," she managed just as Gilli, who had dispensed with her card and been busily tearing the cellophane off her box, spilled pieces of candy across her father's lap.

"Whoa!" he said, frowning, but then Gilli threw her arms around his neck, her mouth stuffed with the one piece of chocolate she'd managed to get her hands on. His expression froze, but the poignancy that shone from his brown eyes squeezed Anna's foolish heart.

Suddenly, she felt like that needy little girl again, the one who would do anything to be noticed, to prove that she was wanted. Slightly panicked and feeling terribly conspicuous, Anna shot to her feet, juggling her portfolio with Reeves's shocking gift. She hadn't even read the card yet. Curiosity all but burned a hole in her brain, but she could not bring herself to open that envelope in company.

"I—I have to run. It's been..." For one horrible moment, her mind went totally blank, but then Reeves dropped his gaze, beginning to help Gilli pick up the candy pieces and return them to the box. As if released from some invisible grip, Anna's thoughts began to whir again. "It's been quite a morning."

"Oh, don't hurry off, Anna Miranda dear," Odelia urged.

"Actually," Reeves put in, his gaze carefully averted, "I think she prefers to be called just plain Anna these days." His eyes met hers then. "Isn't that so, Anna?"

For some insane reason she said, "All my best friends do.

C-call me Anna, that is." She could have kicked herself for saying such an inane thing. "I—I really have to go."

"I'll walk you out," Hypatia said, starting to rise.

"No, no." Anna moved swiftly toward the entry hall. "I know the way. Enjoy your tea before it gets cold. I'll be in touch."

She practically ran from the room, relieved that Hypatia sank back down into her chair. As she made her escape, one crazy notion kept circulating through Anna's mind. Reeves Leland had bought her a Valentine's Day gift. *Reeves Leland* had bought her a Valentine's Day gift.

Her heart pounding, she rushed home to her apartment and feverishly let herself inside. Tossing her keys into a bowl atop a plant stand near the door, she dumped the portfolio in the single chair that comprised her living room furniture before carrying the card and candy box to the drawing board that took up the majority of the space. Carefully, Anna peeled back the flap of the envelope and pulled the card free.

It was a thank-you card.

Tamping down her disappointment, she peeled the cellophane from the candy box and lifted off the lid. She popped a chocolate piece into her mouth. As orange cream melted on her tongue, she mused that at least the card had a heart of pink lace and a bouquet of yellow and blue flowers on the front. Plus, to be fair, the sentiment was appropriate. She opened the card and read it aloud around the remnants of the chocolate.

"You did a thoughtful thing when you didn't have to, and your efforts are greatly appreciated. God bless you." It was signed, "Reeves Kyle Leland."

The doofus had signed it with his full name, as if there might have been another Reeves in the room. Why were men so stupid? Every man she had ever known was clueless, not that she'd known very many.

Anna picked another candy from the box and let her

thumb sink into its middle, cracking the chocolate shell to reveal the pink cream inside. The faint aroma of strawberries teased her nose. She slipped the candy into her mouth, taste buds exploding with chocolate and strawberry, and looked around at the cramped little apartment, which was all she could afford on her meager salary.

With a living room turned studio, despite the sagging, slip-covered chair in the corner, and a kitchen the size of a linen closet, she mostly lived in her bedroom, which made entertaining problematic, not that she had much company. Most of her women friends were married now and starting families, and she made sure to keep the few men she dated well away from here.

Pensively sucking the tip of her thumb clean, Anna folded the card and slid it back into its envelope. As she picked another chocolate from the box, she told herself that it did not matter that the card lacked any romantic sentiment. The days when Reeves Kyle Leland had been a hero to her were long gone. Now he was just an acquaintance, an oblivious father with a little girl too much like herself. If the yawning pit of longing inside her felt unhappily reminiscent of high school, well, Anna knew better than to expect that to have changed. It would be enough, she told herself, if they could just be friends. It would, in fact, be more than she had any reason to hope for.

Reeves pushed away his plate and sat back in his chair, his gaze going to his daughter, seated opposite him next to Odelia. Aunt Mags occupied the chair beside him, while Hypatia, naturally, sat at the head of the massive Renaissance Revival table, leaving the foot and six more chairs empty. Running a finger along the gadrooned edge of the table, Reeves tried not to listen to the *clunk, clunk, clunk* of Gilli's shoes against the stylized Corinthian column that supported the dark, parquet top. She had been a perfect little darling all through dinner, and he hated to upset the applecart by reprimanding her for kicking the table leg with her rubber-toed tennies. It wasn't as if she was doing damage to the table. For some reason, though, his nerves had been on edge all evening, as if the world had unexpectedly shifted on its axis and thrown everything off balance.

He had felt this way once before. That had been the day when Marissa had announced that she was not ready for a child, despite the fact that she was pregnant. She had proposed that they "put off" parenthood. In one horrific moment, he had realized how fundamentally selfish his wife was and that his feelings for her had irrevocably changed. Why he should think of that now, though, he couldn't imagine. It wasn't as if anything had really changed today. Sure, Gilli had learned to skate, but why should that rock his world? Yet, something was different. It was as if a cavern had opened in the floor of the ocean, sucked up all the water and spewed it out again in another direction.

He stared at his daughter, trying to figure out what had happened. She looked up from her plate and smiled, her mouth full of buttered brioche. He thought about correcting her table manners but didn't.

"I have dessert now, Daddy?"

He sat forward and made a show of assessing her plate, which had been picked almost clean despite the cookies and chocolate on which she had dined earlier. "Okay."

"You did very well," Odelia praised her.

Gilli beamed. "I get one piece, don't I, Daddy?"

Nodding, he watched as Hypatia produced that one piece of airy chocolate and crisp rice. Gilli gobbled it down.

"What do you say?" Reeves coached automatically.

To his surprise, she ran around the table and threw herself against him, crying, "Thank you!"

All the water in the ocean rushed back into that undersea cavern. He felt as helpless against it as a piece of flotsam wafting to the ocean floor, waiting to be thrown willy-nilly in a direction it had never traveled before.

Awkwardly, he patted his daughter's back, suggesting, "Why don't you go play until bath time, hmm?"

She ran out of the room without another word or a backward glance.

"I knew Anna Miranda would be good for her," Odelia gushed.

Whoosh! The tide spewed and flung him blindly out to sea. He cleared his throat, shifted in his seat and tried to keep his voice level and casual. "Learning to skate certainly seems to have given Gilli a sense of accomplishment."

"And it's Anna, dear," Hypatia reminded her sister gently.

"Oh. Yes. Amazing what a little time and patient instruction can accomplish with one so young," Odelia went on. "Who'd have thought it? *Anna* was just brilliant with Gilli today. Don't you agree, Reeves?"

He opened his mouth but couldn't find a thing to say that wouldn't drown him, so he closed it again and tilted his head in what might have been construed as a nod. But how, he wondered, could Anna Miranda Burdett be a good influence on his impressionable daughter? Okay, she'd been right about it being time to teach Gilli to skate, though Reeves still privately marveled that anyone could get Gilli to concentrate long enough to do something as physically complicated as skating. That did not mean that Anna knew more about his daughter than he. Did it?

Odelia apparently thought so. "If ever a woman was born to understand a child," she pressed on, "it's Anna Miranda and Gilli." No one corrected her use of Anna's full name this time.

Reeves felt as if he was choking. "Excuse me," he said, dropping his napkin onto his plate. "I'd better check on Gilli."

He left the dining room as sedately as he could manage, despite feeling as if he was being dragged down into that undersea cavern again. Only God knew when and where the unmanageable sea of difficulties that was his life would spit him up next time, but he had the unsettling feeling that wherever that new shore might be, Anna Miranda Burdett would be there waiting. Worse, he feared that Odelia just might be right about her. But, if Anna was actually good for his daughter, then what did that make him?

The problem, he decided. That made him the problem. Just as Marissa had said.

Maybe, he told himself bleakly, it would be best if Marissa did take over raising their daughter. If only he could convince himself that Marissa really cared for Gilli and not whatever financial support might come with her. He just didn't know what was best anymore, and he wasn't sure now that he ever had.

"Nooooo!" Gilli twisted and pulled, trying to free herself of Reeves's hold as he divested her of her coat.

"Cut it out now," Reeves scolded, keeping his voice pitched low. "You know you have to go to Sunday school."

"I don't want to!"

Somehow he'd expected her good behavior to carry over from the day before, but she'd been fighting him all morning, first over what to eat for breakfast and then over getting dressed. Gilli insisted that she hated the dark green velvet and black satin dress that Aunt Mags had given her for Christmas, but it was a cold-weather dress that was already too small, and Reeves figured that if she didn't wear it now, she wouldn't get to wear it at all, which would undoubtedly hurt Magnolia's feelings. After he'd gotten Gilli outfitted in black tights, black patent leather shoes and the abhorred dress, he'd had to badger her into the very coat that she didn't want to take off now. He simply could not fathom what her problem was today.

Glancing around at the families passing through the

hallway of the children's education wing, Reeves wondered why his daughter had to be the only one to balk at going into her class. She had done so almost since she'd been promoted to the three-year-old room six weeks ago. To calm her, he released his grip on her coat but blocked her flight with his body, trapping her against the wall.

"Gilli, you have to go in."

"I wanna stay with you."

Frustration boiled up in him. "You're just being silly," he told her sharply. "I'm sure you'll have fun. Now get in there and enjoy yourself!"

A derisive chuckle had him turning his head. Anna Miranda—rather, *Anna*—stood with arms folded not a yard away. "You figure that's going to work, Stick?"

Overwhelmed and disappointed by the events of the morning, he used his most repressive tone, the one that made his subordinates gulp. "Excuse me?"

Clearly unimpressed, Anna dropped her arms and sauntered closer. "In my experience, you can't just order someone to enjoy themselves."

He felt his face heat. Okay, technically, she was right, but she didn't understand what he'd been through that morning or the resulting level of his frustration. Where had all the amity between him and his daughter gone? Dredging up his driest tone, he drawled, "No? Really? So good of you to share that. Considering you don't have a clue about what's going on here."

"No?"

"No."

Anna parked her hands on her hips, and suddenly he realized that she wore a sweater dress the exact color of blue as her eyes, as well as a pair of tall, sleek black boots. Both left just her shapely knees bare. That dress, modest as it was, left no doubt as to her womanly shape, and Reeves found that it required conscious effort to resist the alarming impulse to step closer.

Something of his thoughts must have shown in his expression, for she instantly bristled. "What's your problem?"

Reeves tried to cover his disturbing fascination with a frown. "I don't have one, other than my daughter not wanting to go into her Sunday school class."

Gilli, who had been staring through the window behind them into the busy, colorful room beyond, tugged on his sleeve. "Daddy, I wanna stay with *you.*"

"Gilli, you know that's not going to happen!" he snapped, at the end of his patience, especially with Anna standing there rolling her eyes.

"And you say I'm the one without a clue," Anna drawled.

Very deliberately, she looked around him and through the large window at the state-of-the-art play area. Over the years, the church had expanded into all of one whole block of the downtown square surrounding the historic county courthouse. On Sunday, it literally took over the downtown area. The one-hundred-and-thirty-year-old sanctuary and the circa 1930s facade on the rest of the buildings in the church plant might have historic significance, but the rabbit warren of rooms in the sprawling complex included easily reconfigurable spaces and all the modern amenities.

Going down on one knee, Anna beckoned Gilli closer and whispered into her ear. Gilli nodded, and Anna whispered again.

"It will?" Gilli asked.

"Mmm-hmm. I bet the other kids will laugh," Anna said, "and everybody likes to laugh, don't you think?"

Giggling, Gilli nodded, then she ran to the half-door and knocked at it. A teacher appeared, smiling down at her. Too relieved to question this about-face, Reeves rushed over to facilitate the process of signing her in. Seconds later, he was waving goodbye to his daughter. Stepping aside, he turned back to Anna with as much annoyance as amazement. How could she manage Gilli when he couldn't?

"I don't know what that was all about, but thanks."

Anna shrugged, her lips curving into a wry smile. "You just have to know what bothers a kid and how to have a little fun with it."

"This morning everything has bothered Gilli," Reeves grumbled.

Anna spread her hands. "So you stuck her in that tight, uncomfortable dress as punishment?"

"No!" Stung, Reeves glared and told her stiffly, "For your information, Aunt Mags bought Gilli that dress for Christmas." He heard giggles from the room behind him but ignored them.

"That doesn't make the dress any more comfortable, you know," Anna argued.

"Well, Gilli seems perfectly happy with it now," he pointed out smartly.

Anna smirked. "Sure she is. I told her what a dress like that is good for."

"And that is?"

"Showing off. Getting people to notice. Especially upside down."

Confused, Reeves shook his head. "Upside down?"

Anna gestured toward the window. "They've got the equivalent of a jungle gym in there, you know."

Reeves whirled around and with very little effort caught sight of his daughter—hanging upside down by her knees from a crossbar on the play station, her skirt covering her face, her ruffled bottom exposed. A crowd of children had gathered around her, laughing and pointing. Horrified, he rounded on Anna.

"You told her to do that?"

Thankfully, the hall had emptied of all but an older gentleman doing duty as a greeter at a side door some distance away. Nevertheless, Reeves lowered his voice, stepping closer to make himself heard. "What were you thinking, telling her to do that?"

"I was thinking," Anna retorted, meeting him nose to nose, "that you wanted her to go into that room without pitching a fit."

Her eyelashes, he noticed, were as bright as brass beneath a thin layer of brown mascara, and why he should find that so infuriatingly intriguing he could not imagine.

"I didn't want her to expose herself in front of the whole class!" Reeves hissed, dropping his gaze and reaching for the doorknob.

Anna intercepted his hand. He jerked back, feeling scorched.

"Will you calm down?" Anna gritted out. "She's three, for pity's sake, and all she's exposed is her ruffled tights. Besides, the teacher's already taken care of it."

He peered through the window again in time to see a woman setting Gilli on her feet and brushing down her skirt. As he watched, a set of blond, freckle-faced twin girls bracketed Gilli, laughing behind their hands. The teacher shepherded them, chattering animatedly, toward a circle forming around another woman with a storybook.

"And look," Anna said, "she's made a couple of friends."

It suddenly occurred to Reeves that he did not know any of these kids, which meant that Gilli probably didn't know any of them, either. Now that he thought about it, he realized that only Gilli and one or two others had been old enough to move up at the beginning of the year. No wonder she had balked at going in. She probably didn't have any friends there. Knowing Gilli, she'd most likely been sitting in a corner all these weeks with her arms folded and her bottom lip stuck out, a sullen, silent, unhappy little stranger. He watched Gilli whisper to her new friends, a gleam in her eye, and sighed inwardly. Turning, he stared down at Anna.

Why was it that he was always the clueless one and Anna always had to be right where *his* daughter was concerned? Still, to tempt Gilli to hang by her knees in Sunday school while wearing a dress.... It was just so *Anna Miranda* and did not seem to bode well for the future.

"She won't always be three, you know," he pointed out.

"But you won't have to drag her kicking and screaming into class next week," Anna rebutted smugly.

Considering how happy Gilli seemed, Reeves imagined that Anna was right about that, too. Still... "And when she's fourteen and desperate to be popular, do I advise her, in your considered opinion, to show her bottom and play the class clown?"

Anna waved that away with a flick of one wrist. "Oh, please. It was just about having a little fun. That's what kids do."

"Is that what you were doing all those years?" he challenged, folding his arms. "Having a little fun at everyone else's expense?"

All expression left Anna's face, but then she lifted her chin and narrowed her eyes at him. "Shouldn't you be in a class somewhere, too?"

He started slightly, remembering time and place. "Yes. And so should you. We can continue this conversation after worship."

"Don't hold your breath waiting for that," Anna said, dancing away, that old cocky insouciance in place once more. "I have a class of six-year-olds to manage, then I'm off to brunch."

"You teach the six-year-olds?" he asked skeptically.

Walking backward, she explained, "Every now and then I substitute for a friend. Why? Don't you think I can handle a six-year-old as well as a three-year-old?"

"Well, yes, but that's not the point."

"Then what is?"

"It's just that I never see you in worship."

"I don't go."

"You teach Sunday school, but you don't stay for worship?"

"Never."

Reeves could not resist following her. "Why not?"

Anna grinned and baldly admitted, "Because it would give my grandmother entirely too much pleasure." She moved on down the hall, winked at the greeter and pushed through a door into a classroom.

Reeves stood where he was, wondering how could she be so right and so wrong at the same time. She dutifully taught children's Sunday school but wouldn't stay for worship because it would please her grandmother. She convinced Gilli to happily go into class and at the same time coached her to make a spectacle of herself. What kind of sense did that make? None, Reeves concluded, which just proved that Anna had never completely grown up. In some ways, he realized, heading toward the men's Bible study class, some part of her would always be a brat, and that made the woman a maddening puzzle, one moment clever and kind, the next irrational and immature. So that meant that one minute the aunties might be right about Anna being a good for Gilli, and the next the opposite might true. Now how was he supposed to deal with that?

He simply did not know what to think of Anna Burdett or how to feel about her. He did know this much: By letting Tansy drive her away from the worship service, Anna was as good as cutting off her nose to spite her face. Everyone needed a healthy personal relationship with God Almighty through Jesus Christ, and that meant regularly being in worship. Someone had to make Anna see that.

Of course, he was not that someone. Why, he was the last person for the job.

But if not me, then who? he wondered.

Shaking his head, Reeves told himself that God would bring the right person along. He just didn't want to think that maybe He already had.

Smoothing the ruffled edge of a pink skirt with the tip of one finger, Anna tilted her head to study the drawing, her toe tapping along with the lively beat of a favorite rock song. She loved working with pastels, but it had been weeks since she'd last pulled them out. Her encounter that morning with Reeves and Gilli had left her feeling oddly unsettled, so it was inevitable that she should turn to her secret passion as a way to center herself. She strove to tell a story with each picture, imagining how other fertile imaginations might interpret her drawings.

A knock at the door had her first looking up in surprise then checking the time via the digital display on the small, inexpensive stereo system atop the cheap shelving unit tucked into a corner next to the tiny bar that separated the tiny kitchen from the tiny living/studio area. As it was just past noon, the hour at which Downtown Bible Church turned out, Anna had a hunch that Tansy knocked at her door. Sighing, she got up and went to find out. It was too late, with music pumping out of the stereo, to pretend to be gone. Sure enough, her grandmother pushed into the room the instant that the door cracked open, her patent leather handbag dangling by the strap from one elbow.

"Well, hi there, Tansy," Anna deadpanned, taking on a dual role. "Hello, Anna. Won't you come in, Tansy? Why, thank you, Anna. How nice of you to ask."

Tansy ignored this completely, just stood there in heavy pumps that, naturally, matched the handbag. The navy patent leather seemed a bit much with the casual style of her dark blue knit pants and flowered rayon blouse, but it was quintessential Tansy. Turning in a circle, Tansy's critical gaze swept the tightly confined space. Even strict organization could not keep it from appearing cluttered and messy, but Anna would not defend herself on that or any point.

"Ginger Elkanor had her baby last night," Tansy announced baldly. "Girl. Thought you'd want to know."

"Thanks," Anna said drily. "I'm aware." Actually, it was for Ginger that Anna had substituted that morning, not that she wanted her grandmother to know about that.

"Since it's the second child, there won't be a shower," Tansy went on, "but that doesn't mean her friends shouldn't take over a gift."

As if Anna could not decipher that for herself. She glanced at the illustration on her drawing board, murmuring, "I thought I'd frame one of my drawings. That would at least be unique."

"Unique," Tansy huffed, a familiar expression of disapproval on her face. "Unique is overrated. Besides, what would an infant need with a drawing? Buy her a bag of disposable diapers. Now that's useful."

"Useful but boring."

Tansy rolled her eyes. "That's the trouble with you, Anna Miranda. You think life ought to be entertaining, fun. When are you going to act responsibly, settle down and have a family of your own?"

Now that Tansy's excuse for this visit was out of the way, Anna mused, the old girl could get about her real business of running Anna's life, or trying to. Anna had to give it to Tansy. She never quit, a trait she shared with her granddaughter.

"And give up all this?" Anna quipped, holding out her hands. "What makes you think I want a family, anyway? All family's ever been to me is a pain."

"You want to talk about pain? What about the pain of losing my only son?"

"He's been dead for over twenty-five years," Anna pointed out softly.

"And his father for ten years before that, but do you ever think about the pain I've suffered because of it? What about the pain and embarrassment you've caused with your behavior?" Tansy went on. "All I've ever wanted is what's best for you."

"That and to control my every breath," Anna sniped.

"Will you be serious for once!" Tansy demanded. "And

if you're going to listen to that ridiculous music, at least turn it down!"

Anna went straight to the stereo and turned up the volume a notch.

Tansy marched over and punched the power button on the stereo as if Anna was ten and they did not stand in *her* home. Anna glared through the silence that followed.

"You're going to ruin your hearing," Tansy said defensively.

"It's *my* hearing. I'll ruin it if I want to," Anna snapped, aware that she was reverting to her sixteen-year-old self but unable to stop. "You have no right to touch things in *my* apartment!"

Tansy frowned sourly. Stomping to the door, she muttered, "Just once I'd like to have a normal conversation with you. Just once!"

As Tansy went out, Anna spun around and slapped the power button on the stereo with one hand, wrenching up the volume with the other. Anna was still heaving in angry breaths when the neighbors next door began to beat on the wall. Instantly, Anna lashed out by spinning the volume knob all the way up. Then, for some reason, Reeves came to mind. In a flash, she imagined him watching from afar, like God on high peering down from lofty realms. Anna turned down the volume, feeling foolish and immature and…sad.

After a moment, her raging heartbeat slowed, but the sick feeling in the pit of her stomach remained. She sat down at her drawing table and began ruthlessly "correcting" her work. After a long while, she sat back to take a critical view. It came as no surprise that the little girl in that ruffled pink skirt bore a decided resemblance to Gilli Leland.

Chapter Six

"Anna was at church this morning?" Odelia asked breathlessly, clapping her hands together. She barely missed catching the tips of her long, dangling earrings. They looked like bunches of grapes swaying above the dining table. "How wonderful! I'm sorry I missed her."

Reeves forked a bite of omelet into his mouth—the aunties ate so-called "simple fare" on Sundays—and shook his head. "She didn't stay for worship. She was just there to substitute for a teacher in the six-year-old department."

Her fork poised in midair, Hypatia sighed. "I worry about that girl."

"What girl?" Gilli asked, butter all over her face from the triangle of toast in her hand. "I know two girls, Elizbet and Mogumry." She scrunched up her face, adding, "But I don't know what one they are."

Reeves smiled. "You must mean the twins I saw this morning." Obviously, Gilli couldn't tell them apart. Their mother surely had not named them Elizabeth and Montgomery, though. Had she?

"I meant Anna, dear," Hypatia clarified for the child, adding mildly, "Don't wipe your mouth on your sleeve. You'll ruin your pretty blouse."

"It gots ruffles," Gilli announced proudly, holding out her arms.

"Say, 'Yes, ma'am,'" Reeves coached, fixing her with a level look.

Defiantly, she bit off a huge chunk of bread instead, replacing the butter that she'd just wiped off her face with her sleeve. Reeves counted to ten, tamping down his temper as Gilli chewed, as soon as she swallowed, he leaned forward and removed the remaining bread from her plate.

"Yes, ma'am. Or we trade the ruffles for a plain T-shirt."

Ruffles suddenly had taken on a monumental importance in Gilli's life. Since this morning's escapade, she had talked ruffles almost nonstop. She'd even insisted on wearing that white blouse when Reeves had helped her change out of her church clothes before lunch.

"Yes, ma'am," she muttered.

Apparently hanging upside down by her knees to show off the ruffled bottoms of her tights had made her a minor celebrity with the three-year-old set, and so ruffles must now be the predominant feature of her wardrobe. Reeves still was not thrilled about that episode, but Gilli had been so happy since then that he couldn't bring himself to lecture her on the subject. Besides, he reasoned, Anna was to blame, not Gilli.

"About Anna," Odelia said thoughtfully, picking up the thread of the conversation. "I wonder why she doesn't attend worship."

Reeves put the bread back on Gilli's plate. She snatched it up and took another big bite. "I believe it has to do with her grandmother," Reeves revealed absently. "Anna said it would please Tansy too much if she went to worship."

Hypatia frowned. "Surely she didn't mean that."

"Surely she did," Mags muttered, "and who could blame her? You know how Tansy is. Let her think she's won on one issue, she'll try to run everything."

"Well, it's not right," Hypatia pointed out. Reeves had

thought the same thing, but he wisely kept his mouth closed. He was glad of it when Hypatia said, "Someone has to speak to Anna about this."

"Not that she would listen to us," Odelia said innocently. "Why would a girl, er, young woman like her care what three old biddies like us might say?"

"I take issue with being called an old biddy," Hypatia sniffed, "but you're entirely right about the other. She needs to hear it from someone nearer her own age."

Reeves shifted in his chair, uncomfortably aware where this was headed.

Mags pointed her knife at him. "Maybe you should do it, nephew. Maybe you could make Anna see what a mistake she's making by not attending worship."

Just because he had known it was coming didn't mean he had to like it.

"Me?" he asked indignantly. "What makes you think she'd listen to me? Why should I be the one?"

Mags went back to cutting a slice of tomato with a steak knife. "If not you," she asked, stabbing him straight through the conscience, "then who?"

Reeves stared at her for a good ten seconds as his own thought from that morning returned to pour salt into the wound. Bowing his head, he surrendered in silence. God didn't have to crack his skull with a two-by-four. Ruffles and a steak knife were quite enough. He would say something as soon as the right moment presented itself. Now if only Anna would listen, but why should she?

He hadn't exactly been amiable and personable with her. Most of the time he'd been downright rude. He was going to have to mend his ways, make friends with her, if that was possible. At the very least, he was going to have to be polite.

Okay, Lord, if that's what You want, then You're going to have to help me. Big time.

* * *

Pleased with the new fuel contract that he had just successfully negotiated, Reeves stepped up into the charming little bistro with the Director of Operations at his side. Their hard work had been rewarded with nice bonuses, and they'd decided to celebrate at Buffalo Creek's most popular café. Considering that the morning had started with a telephone call from his ex, the day had definitely improved; yet, he couldn't quite get that call off his mind.

Marissa had taken up residence in San Antonio and wanted, she'd said, to give him her new address. She had complained that she wasn't earning enough to make ends meet and insisted that they needed to "rethink their divorce agreement." Otherwise, she had said, she'd have to find another way to "make an adequate home for Gilli." He had pointed out that she'd never stated any intention of making any sort of home for Gilli before, to which she had retorted, "Things change."

He knew a threat when he heard one, but his ready cash was tied up in house repairs and would be until the last of the insurance came through. If he'd had the bonus money then, he might have given that to her, though it was just as well she did not have the means to hire an attorney or open court proceedings, not that he seriously thought she would do so. Every time she reached out, though, he was forcibly reminded of his inadequacies and failures. But not today, he decided. Today he was going to hold this one small triumph close and forget about all the rest.

That proved easier than he'd expected when he spied Anna at a table with an older couple across the way. The man looked vaguely familiar, but he knew that he'd never seen the woman before. She said something, and Anna laughed, putting her head back to let the sound roll up out of her throat in a rich, musical flow. The instant that she saw him, the laughter stopped. Reminded forcefully of his conversation with God on Sunday past, he put on a smile and was rewarded with a look of genuine welcome. He found that welcoming expression compelling, so as the waitress showed him and his companion to their table, he excused himself to briefly detour in Anna's direction.

The vibrant yellow-orange walls, painted with trailing vines and birds nesting in tree branches, provided a fetching backdrop for Anna's golden beauty, Reeves mused as he walked across the black-and-white checkerboard floor. Once he arrived at the table, however, he found himself appallingly bereft of conversation beyond, "Hello."

Anna, fortunately, had no such problem. "Come here often?"

It sounded like the worst of pickup lines, and he almost laughed, as she no doubt intended. Instead, he cleared his throat. "Not really, no."

"Special occasion then?"

"Business thing," he said, nodding.

Both of Anna's eyebrows lifted. "The negotiations must have gone well."

"You knew about that?"

"Your aunts mentioned something about it." Effectively changing the subject, she looked to the couple with her. "You may not remember Howard from the print shop."

"But I do," Reeves said, shaking hands with the older man.

"And this is his wife Lois."

"Ma'am."

"They have a special occasion, too," Anna announced.

Lois, whose slate brown, shoulder-length hair was sprinkled with silver, hunched her plump shoulders and cast a loving gaze on her husband. "Twenty-eight years."

"Your wedding anniversary?" Reeves surmised.

Leaning sideways, she linked her arm with her husband's. "Yes. Anna's treating us to lunch in celebration."

"Congratulations. That's quite an accomplishment."

Harold smiled and patted his wife's hand. "Sadly, these days it is, but then there aren't many like my Lois."

"Oh, you shameless old flirt," Lois teased. She winked at Anna and quipped, "He just keeps me around because I make him laugh."

"Hey, a man with a sense of humor is a rare find," Anna returned. "Take it from me. I would know. Right, Stick?"

He didn't know what to say to that, so he just smiled. "Well, I don't want to keep my friend waiting." He nodded to Howard and Lois. "Nice to meet you folks. Anna."

"Enjoy your lunch."

"Thanks. You, too." He started to turn away, but then he stopped, remembering that he had a mission where Anna was concerned. For a moment, he was unsure what to do. He didn't think it wise to say that he wanted to talk to her about church. Then he remembered something. "Actually," he said, "I meant to tell you that Gilli's been asking about you."

Anna brightened. "Oh?"

Relieved in a way that he couldn't quite identify, Reeves smiled and nodded. Gilli *had* asked when Anna would come and skate with her again, prompting Reeves to walk out onto the back patio with her to watch her demonstrate her newly acquired skating skills. She hadn't asked after Anna since. Indeed, that simple gesture on his part had seemed to have pleased his little girl mightily, which had, in turn, humbled him. He was beginning to realize how much he'd left to the nanny, more than he should have. Much more. In some ways, he was only now getting to know his daughter.

"She'd like it if you stopped by to say hello sometime," he went on carefully.

"I'll make a point of it," Anna said. "I have to call on your aunts soon, anyway."

"We'll look forward to it." The seed of a future conversation planted, Reeves seemed to have run out of words for this one again. He flipped a wave and walked away, leaving Anna smiling as if he'd given her something precious, something more than just a friendly word. It made him feel small to think that he might have given her that at any point in the past.

He could not remember when he'd taken an early weekend, Reeves thought, turning the sedan into the drive of Chatam House that following Friday a good three hours before his usual quitting time. The gate, featuring a large copperplate *C* at its center, stood open in welcome as usual. He could count on one hand the number occasions, in his memory, that it had been closed. Perhaps that perpetual welcome was one reason why he so looked forward to coming home. God knew that Chatam House felt more like home to him now than the house that he had shared with Marissa ever had.

He pushed away thoughts of her and her increasingly shrill demands, steering the sedan around to the west side of the house. Strangely unsurprised to find Anna's battered old coupe parked beneath the porte cochere there, he parked next to it and got out. He *was* surprised to find Anna and Gilli sitting cross-legged on the ground at the edge of the drive tossing pebbles at the massive magnolia tree on the west lawn. The waxy, palm-sized, evergreen leaves had turned brown around the edges due to the cold, but Reeves knew that they would not fall from the stems until new foliage appeared in the spring, unless they were knocked free by, for example, flying gravel.

He walked toward them, pleased when Gilli smiled and waved at him. Anna glanced his way, then picked a small stone from the edge of the drive and tossed it into the tree. What fell to the dirt was not a large, leathery leaf, as expected, but a scrawny gray cat, yowling in surprised protest. Gilli gasped, and for a second the entire tableau froze. Then, suddenly, both Anna and Gilli burst out laughing. An instant later, the cat streaked around the converted carriage house, where the staff lived, and out of sight.

"It was a cat!" Gilli exclaimed needlessly. "We got a cat, Daddy!"

He didn't bother correcting her. The cat was long gone, after all.

Sobered, Anna said, "I hope I didn't hurt it."

"It looked okay to me, just surprised."

"No more surprised than us," she replied with a chuckle.

"Anna knocked off a cat!" Gilli exclaimed, laughing. Suddenly she looked up at him. "I can knock off leaves, Daddy. Watch!"

Anna sent him a telling glance, even as she too reached for a pebble—from behind Gilli. "Slow and easy," she counseled, glancing up at him again, this time with a conspiratorial look in her eyes.

Gilli took aim, holding her pebble no higher than her nose. Then suddenly her arm shot up, and she threw it. At the same time, Anna flung her stone up from the ground and over Gilli's head. Gilli's pebble traveled about ten feet, plopping silently and unseen, by her at least, to the right. Anna's sailed into the tree about midway up, and a pair of leaves rattled slowly to the ground beneath.

"I got two! I got two!" Gilli crowed.

"Beans!" Anna complained. "That makes you the winner."

Gilli radiated delight even as she comforted Anna with a pat on her knee. "Uh-uh. You knocked off the cat. 'Member?"

Anna snorted. It sounded suspiciously like a strangled laugh.

Abruptly, Reeves wanted to reach down and scoop them both into his arms. He wanted to savor the whole moment, including the mute byplay with Anna. He had known, somehow, what she was planning, what she had been doing, for Gilli all along, and it warmed his heart, especially when Gilli seemed so pleased with her supposed pebble-tossing prowess. Rattled by these unexpected emotions, he nevertheless wanted Anna to know how grateful he was, despite his doubts sometimes about her methods and the sudden envy that he felt because Gilli never laughed so easily with him. That, he knew, was his own fault, and he meant, somehow, to remedy the situation.

Anna pushed up from the ground, her long, slender legs straightening to show off the snug, easy fit of her nut-brown corduroy jeans, which she wore with a quilted tan jacket and long, colorful striped wool scarf.

"I better get a move on," she said, and the sound of her voice made him realize that he'd been staring. Quickly, he dropped his gaze, nodding.

"Don't go, Anna," Gilli pleaded. "Stay and knock off leaves with us."

"I can't, sweetie," Anna said. "I still haven't seen your aunts, and I need to get back to work soon. Unfortunately."

Reeves seized on that. "Don't you like your job?"

She grimaced. "I like the work, at least."

"You should. You're quite good at it."

Her eyebrows lifted. A moment later, she bowed her head as if trying to hide the smile that curled her lips. "Yeah, well, to tell you the truth, my boss is a bit of a bear. Kind of takes the fun out of things, you know, but I like working with Howard."

"He seems very nice."

"He is, and that makes dealing with Dennis easier."

Reeves found himself reaching for some way to help her. "Maybe you ought to consider changing jobs anyway. There are bound to be opportunities in Dallas."

She shook her head, already moving away. "I wouldn't know how to even begin looking."

He didn't want her to leave. That nonsensical, rather alarming thought took him by surprise. He immediately rationalized it. How was he supposed to talk to her about getting back into the habit of attending worship service if they never spent any time together? Before he could think of a way to make that happen, she called out, "Gotta go. See you guys later."

Gilli folded her arms, pout in full force, but then she turned a beseeching face up at him. "Wanna play? Wanna knock off leaves with me, Daddy? Please? Pleeease."

Gilli had never asked him to play before. Maybe she hadn't realized that adults could play, or maybe that was just one more essential that he'd left to the nanny. He looked back over his shoulder, watching Anna disappear around the corner of the house, then he carefully lowered himself to the ground. Gilli's happy laughter curled around him like tendrils of incense. Was this how God felt about the happiness of His children? Reeves hoped so.

"I wonder if I can knock off a dog," he teased, reaching back to pick up a handful of pebbles.

Gilli giggled. "Daaady! Dogs don't go in trees!"

"No? Hmm. We'll see." He let loose with the pebble in his hand. It sailed high into the tree, but the leaf that he knocked free failed to make it to the ground, caught somewhere in the jumble of limbs.

Gilli couldn't believe it. Her elbows braced on her knees, she turned up her palms. Then she gasped and wonder lit her face as she whispered, "Maybe the dog gots it!"

Grinning, Reeves looked back to the tree, calling, "Hey, pooch! Fetch me my leaf." Without Gilli realizing it, he threw another pebble, aiming for the middle limbs this time, and a single leaf fell straight to the ground. Gilli's eyes popped big as saucers. "Good, pooch," Reeves said, winking.

"Daaady!"

She fell against him, laughing, and when he put his arm around her, joy suffused him. He almost felt sorry for Marissa. Despite all of her declarations about making a home for Gilli, she hadn't even asked how their daughter was or said anything about arranging a visit. All she'd talked about was needing money. She had no idea what she was really missing.

It occurred to him that Anna was nothing like Marissa. She obviously didn't have much, and she just as obviously didn't expect much. For another thing, she was good with Gilli, better than any nanny he had ever hired. She actually seemed to like his daughter and spending time with her. The aunties were right. Not only did she seem to understand Gilli better than her own mother did, Anna seemed to understand Gilli better than her father. That was the saddest thing of all. Anna Miranda was a better parent than him or Marissa.

But he was trying, and maybe someday he could change that, once God was through with him, had *fixed* him somehow, made him a better man, a better Christian. Maybe, with the right woman... He dared not ask himself if Anna could be that woman. Yet, she had indisputably given him insight into his daughter, and he thought that perhaps he was a bit better as a father because of it.

The thought occurred to him that he ought to do something for Anna in gratitude. An idea began to form in the back of his mind. But first things first.

"Your turn," he told Gilli, surreptitiously picking up another pebble from the edge of the drive.

Once more, she took careful aim, and a tiny rock plopped into the grass, but she saw only the rusty green leaf that tumbled to the ground as she crowed in celebration.

They spent a good quarter-hour tossing pebbles at the magnolia tree. Later, while she napped, he slipped off on a long run. When he returned to the mansion, she complained about having awakened and found him gone, so he consented to watch a video with her after dinner. As it was Friday, he even allowed her to stay up later than usual. Eventually, she drifted off to sleep, cuddled up next to him on the comfy cream white leather sofa before the fireplace in their suite.

Carrying her to bed, he felt that lately they had made progress. Being at Chatam House helped. His aunties and their faith permeated the place with peace and comfort. Not having the nanny around to take care of things like getting Gilli dressed and bathed had made a big difference, too, more than he could have guessed, but he knew that the lion's share of the credit went to Anna.

She had shown him that Gilli was more than a fussy, irrational baby. Anna had shown him how important it was to pay attention to Gilli and have a little fun with her. As a result, Gilli laughed more, shone more and behaved better. Reeves realized that he'd secretly feared that his daughter hated him, but that was not the case. She needed him; she might even love him. Life wasn't without its frustrations where Gilli was concerned, but he certainly enjoyed her more.

"Thank You, Lord," he whispered, lowering her onto her pillow. He brushed her curls from her forehead and pulled up the downy blanket to tuck it around her. He spent a long time in prayer that night, just being thankful, and he asked for something that had never occurred to him before. He asked to forget the pain of his failed marriage, realizing that it had caused him to ignore in so many ways the one good thing to have come from that catastrophe, his daughter.

They slept in on Saturday then enjoyed a light, simple breakfast together in their suite. Reeves went downstairs and put it together himself, Hilda having moved on to other chores. Gilli was thrilled to discover that he'd sent it up in the old dumbwaiter that opened onto the landing. Later, when he had errands to run, she begged to go along. Despite fearing that she would tire before he had accomplished what he must, he gave in.

Their first stop was the dry cleaners, where he picked up a week's worth of shirts and his tuxedo. He'd dropped off his tux as soon as the aunties had made it clear that this year's fund-raiser was to be a gala affair. He had worn the thing exactly twice in his life, once at his sister's wedding and again at his own. Might as well get some good out of it when he could.

After that, he drove over to the pharmacy to replenish their supply of vitamins. There Gilli demanded a candy bar, but he deflected a confrontation by offering lunch at her favorite pizza place instead, a small concession since he'd planned to eat out anyway. Taking Gilli into the local home improvement store next probably wasn't the smartest move he could have made, which was why he gave up trying to pick out a new light fixture for the kitchen midway through the project. He still had time, he told the beleaguered salesman, who was undoubtedly relieved that he'd gotten rid of them before something ended up broken. Lunch became a rather long, drawn out, fractious affair, but Reeves was pleased that he managed to keep his cool, even though Gilli couldn't seem to sit still in the booth for three minutes running.

Their final stop was their own house, where he inspected the new rafters. While he was up in the attic, Gilli went to her bedroom where she pulled out half a dozen more toys that she wanted to take back to the mansion with her.

"Please, Daddy, please."

Reeves shook his head. "You have plenty of toys at the aunties' house now. Besides we'll be moving back here soon."

She looked positively stricken for a moment, then she did something he hadn't expected. She pitched a crying, screaming fit. "I don't want to! I want my toys! I want my toys!"

Stunned and exasperated, Reeves resorted to the only method that he knew of to cope. He pulled her up and sternly marched her outside to the car, wailing like a banshee. Saddened that their day out had come to this, Reeves drove back to Chatam House in pained silence, letting her wail and rage until, exhausted, she calmed to mere snuffles.

No sooner did he set her feet on the graveled drive,

however, than she bolted, wailing anew. The aunties finally managed to calm her. Reeves knew this because some time after he left them to it, her cries finally faded, and at dinner she, like his aunts, was glum and quiet.

It tore at Reeves heart to think that they had not made as much progress as he had believed, so much so that he actually thought about calling up Anna to discuss it with her. But no, that was the sort of thing one discussed with a wife and partner or, at the very least, a trusted friend and advisor. He would figure this out on his own, somehow, God willing. But how? Oh, Father in heaven, how?

Chapter Seven

Sunday brought little of the angst and frustration that Reeves expected. Gilli morosely donned the dress that he chose for her without serious complaint, though she bemoaned the lack of ruffles on her tights. For his part, he made sure that the dress fit comfortably. He had to bite his tongue to keep from admonishing her not to repeat that upside down business, but in the end it did not seem necessary as the twins were waiting for her when she trudged sullenly through her Sunday school room door. He stood outside the window and watched her for a few minutes, turning away only when she giggled at something one of her new friends said.

He turned half expecting Anna to be there with some sarcastic quip on the tip of her tongue, but he was alone in the hallway except for a couple dropping off their child at the six-year-olds' classroom. He moved that way before he even realized what he was doing. At the door, he heard himself asking if Anna Burdett was teaching today.

"No, she's not part of our team," a young woman told him. "We trade off, every other Sunday, except for the directors. Would you like me to ask them where you could find her?"

He shook his head, already moving away. "It's not important. I'll catch up with her later. Thanks."

Why, he wondered suddenly, instead of looking for the right moment to speak to her about attending worship had he not simply invited her to come to church with him and Gilli? What a simple solution that would have been! On the other hand, inviting Anna to church might presage more than mere Christian concern. He was afraid that he was coming to like her too much.

With a sudden rush of insight, he saw all the ways he had employed to keep from thinking of her. The errands, the meals, television, even arguing with Gilli. He had abdicated a sacred responsibility out of selfish fear.

Guilt swamped him. He owed Anna; not only that, he owed God. The two felt inextricably intwined.

That thought stayed with him throughout the remainder of the day and on into the next morning. Recalling their conversation about her dissatisfaction with her job, he took the time to do some research online concerning opportunities for graphic artists. What he found surprised him, but he wasn't sure what to do with the information, even when he returned to Chatam House that evening to again find Anna's vehicle parked in the drive.

The rich, meaty aroma of Hilda's roast beef welcomed him as he entered, as usual, through the side door. Inhaling deeply, he whispered a prayer of thanksgiving for the feast to come and moved on toward the central hall. Even before he reached the intersection, he could hear Gilli giggling in the sunroom. Making a sharp left, he went straight there.

The aunties occupied their usual seats, Mags and Od on identical chaises, Hypatia in the chair across the way. Next to Hypatia, on her right, sat Anna. Gilli lay draped belly down across Anna's lap.

"Oh! Here's your daddy now," Odelia said, beaming up at Reeves.

Today's earrings glittered like the moon and stars. Actually, on closer inspection, they *were* moons and stars, blue and silver, radiating outward in small, spiral galaxies. The colors perfectly matched her denim jumper and the silvery satin blouse beneath it. Reeves grinned. Auntie Od never failed to delight, bless her.

"Hi, Daddy," Gilli greeted offhandedly. Sliding off Anna's lap to loop an arm around Anna's neck, she announced, "Anna stayin' for dinner."

"Is she?" He forced a smile, feeling a bit off kilter. His heart seemed to be beating too hard. "Someone must have told her that Hilda's serving a roast for dinner tonight."

Anna chuckled. "Let's just say that my nose works perfectly, so no one had to ask me twice."

Hypatia tilted her head back to look up at him. "You have time to change if you'd like, dear."

"I think I'll do that," he decided.

The women went back to their conversation, and he made a quick escape up the stairs, where he traded his suit for jeans and a burgundy pullover. Anna, it seemed, was becoming a fixture around here. Not even the aunties were immune to her quirky charm. He froze, a sense of déjà vu coming over him.

Suddenly he was back in high school, listening to everyone laugh at Anna Miranda's latest nonsense—and secretly burning up with envy. He could never be that clever, that careless, that uninhibited. He could only be stolid, responsible…confused. His mother had once called him "self-contained," as if that was a good thing and did not separate him somehow from everyone else.

He was heartily sick of being contained within himself, bored beyond bearing with the passionless existence he'd created. It was, he realized, how he had protected himself from the chaos of his childhood and the reason he had chosen Marissa, a creature of excessive passions. And wasn't Anna the same?

No, he decided, she wasn't. Her behavior with Gilli demonstrated that, as did her willingness to toil at a job where she was not appreciated, drive a battered old jalopy and accommodate three adorably eccentric old women. Perhaps she was stubborn and clever and glib, but she was also generous and principled in a way that he had never expected.

After stomping into a comfortable pair of old loafers, he hurried back down the stairs to plop into a chair placed at an angle to Anna's. Gilli had stretched out next to Mags on the chaise in the interim and was in the midst of a long story about "her" cat, claiming that it lived in the magnolia tree and a hole in the hedge that rimmed the property on three sides. Mags said that she had seen the thin gray cat around the place several times lately. Hypatia, who had an aversion to cats, shuddered.

Carol came in to announce that dinner was ready, and they all trooped in to take seats at the massive dining table. They made a motley crew, Mags in her scruffy usual, Od at her outrageous best, Hypatia fit for a diplomatic mission in her pearls and elegant suit, him in his jeans and Gilli in a long-sleeved T-shirt and baggy, faded pink pants just a tad too short despite the ruffles around the hems. Anna looked wonderful in black boots, a long, slender black skirt and a black suede vest worn over a soft white blouse with voluminous sleeves cuffed at the wrists. She proved not only a lovely dinner companion but also a very amiable one.

"Thanks to you three and your fund-raiser, my stock has quite risen at the print shop," she said in reply to a question from Hypatia concerning her job. "Why, I suspect that if I hadn't spilled coffee on Dennis's estimates for a new project today I would be enjoying unprecedented job security just now." Cocking her head, she narrowed her eyes. "No, wait, if it's intentional, that's *pouring,* isn't it?" Grinning, she added, "Spilling is *accidental.*"

Odelia twittered behind her hand then asked, "Was it really intentional?"

"Absolutely," Anna said without the least regret. "It was either that, watch a client get unintentionally hosed, or attempt to point out Dennis's glaring mistakes to him."

"Attempt?" Reeves echoed.

She lifted an eyebrow at him. "Hard to see a mistake when you cannot be wrong."

"Ah. I see. You shouldn't have to put up with that."

"Must be tough when it's the boss who's like that," Mags surmised.

Anna shrugged. "Howard and I worked out a system to deal with him."

"Who's Howard?" Mags asked.

"Coworker," she answered succinctly, spearing a piece of browned potato. "I spill—or rather, pour—and when Dennis roars, Howard runs in with a fresh estimate sheet. Dennis rarely even notices the corrections." She ate the potato, musing, "I look at my job like a cat and mouse game. Unfortunately I keep on winding up as the mouse."

"What's cat-n-moufe game?" Gilli wanted to know, concentrating, as usual, on the bread, in this case, hot, fluffy yeast rolls.

Anna shifted slightly to address her. "You know, cartoon stuff, where the cat's always chasing the mouse, and the mouse always manages to get away."

Gilli nodded, laughing. "Oh, yeah. That."

"Hey, did you ever see the one about the skillets?" Anna asked.

She went on to give them a hilarious blow-by-blow account. It went on for a good ten minutes, and no sooner had the laughter died down than Gilli asked, in all innocence, "What's a skillet?"

Anna traded a look with Reeves, a silent communication that felt oddly intimate. He felt the strangest impulse to reach out and take her hand beneath the table, but then, eyes sparkling, she tucked her chin to hide her silent laughter while Hypatia calmly answered.

"It's a pan for cooking in, and much too heavy for a real cat or mouse to lift."

Gilli nodded, offering sagely, "Cartoons is just pretend."

"Indeed, they are," Hypatia replied while everyone else continued to hide smiles.

"What are your favorite cartoons?" Anna asked Gilli, getting a mangled mishmash of description and titles in return. The aunties were lost.

Anna, who seemed quite well informed on the subject, went on to explain and describe each and every one of Gilli's favorite programs. It became apparent to Reeves that the nanny had allowed Gilli to view much more television than he'd have preferred. He made a mental note to police her viewing habits more carefully. A few moments later he noticed that she was nodding over her plate. They had stayed at the table far longer than normal, but it was not yet Gilli's bedtime.

"She refused to take a nap today," Hypatia informed him softly.

"Sat out on the kitchen doorstep with a bowl of milk all day long waiting for that cat," Odelia explained.

"Nearly caught it, too," Mags added proudly.

Reeves got to her feet. "I'd better take her up now."

Gilli roused at that, mumbling, "Anna come."

Reeves looked to Anna. Without even the slightest hesitation, she pushed back her chair, dropping her napkin beside her plate.

"Thank you for a lovely dinner," Anna said to the aunties. "I'll say good-night now, but I'll see you soon. I'll bring the other print goods over as they are finished." She followed him around the table toward Gilli. Bending, he scooped Gilli into his arms. She wrapped all four limbs around him, laying her head on his shoulder.

"Good night, dears," Hypatia said. "Reeves, I trust you'll see Anna out?"

"Uh, sure."

More matchmaking? he wondered, carrying Gilli toward the central hall. He didn't mind as much as he might have.

Anna fell into step beside him. They climbed the stairs side by side, then Reeves led the way along the landing to the open door of the suite. There he motioned Anna to go ahead, knowing that the modern amenities of the suite in this house of antiques would be something of a surprise to her. She didn't try to hide her curiosity or appreciation as she looked around the comfortable sitting room with its cream walls, puffy matching leather couch, thick burgundy rugs and flat screen television hanging over the mantle of the ornate fireplace, all accented with touches of spring green and gold.

He carried Gilli into her bedchamber. As in his own bedroom at the opposite end of the sitting room, the burgundy carried over into the carpeting and drapes here with pale French Provincial furniture and muted spring green linens softening the effect. Only the stuffed animals on the bed, toys scattered around the room in various containers and stacks of books on the dresser identified this as a child's room.

He sat Gilli on the side of the tall bed then went to pull her pajamas from the dresser. Anna moved in and began to undress the weary child. Once she was suitably garbed for bed, Reeves urged her into the small private bath. Freshly washed and brushed, Gilli made no protest as Reeves lifted her up and laid her on the pillows, but as soon as the covers were folded beneath her chin, she began to plead for a story.

"Aw, Gilli, you're exhausted," he argued. "Let's just say our prayers and get to sleep."

"Pleeease, Daddy. Anna will read. Won't you, Anna?"

"I have a better idea," Anna said, going to the dresser to quickly rifle through the books. Finding one she liked, she returned to sit against the headboard and gather Gilli against her. "Let's make up a story." She opened the book and showed

Gilli the first picture. "Hmm," she said, "this bunny looks lost to me. Where do you think she was going? A birthday party, maybe?"

Gilli's eyes lit up. "Yeah, a birthday!"

"I wonder where she'll wind up," Anna murmured, turning the page.

Reeves stood there, listening to the two of them spin a simple story based on the pictures alone. It was nothing like the actual story, which Gilli knew by heart. Why, she could practically recite it, and for that reason he had steadfastly refused to read the thing for days. Now here was Anna patiently, happily breathing new life into one of Gilli's favorite books, and all it took was a little time, attention and imagination.

Gulping, Reeves realized that he normally rushed through the bedtime routine, his mind on the instant when he could take his own ease in private. Yet, what did he do as soon as he closed the door to this room? Too often, he began to dwell on the problems awaiting him at work or rehashed his many failures. Alone and lonely, he routinely cried out to God, begging to be made a better father, nephew, boss, employee, servant, whatever, never facing the fact until now that he failed because he hurried through the most important moments.

Forgive me, Lord, he thought. Then he sat down on the other side of the bed and joined in the story.

Gilli finally giggled herself to a happy ending. Anna closed the book and, following Reeves's example, dropped a kiss on the little curly-top's head. Gilli immediately folded her hands and started to pray.

"God is great, and God is good," the girl began. Anna smiled, for Gilli had begun the mealtime blessing. With a nudge from her father, she started over. "Now I lay me down to sleep..."

After the usual rhyme, Gilli began to thank God. Her list was long, including her daddy, the aunties, grandparents, cousins, many other family members, toys, dolls, skates, books… Eventually she got to the whole earth, sun, sky, trees and so forth. At the very end, she shook Anna to the core.

"And thank You for Anna 'cause You love her, too, and she's my goodest friend. Amen."

"Amen," Reeves echoed, but Anna found that she couldn't speak around the lump in her throat.

Silently, she watched Gilli snuggle down and close her eyes. Slipping from the room, she keenly felt Reeves on her heels. It was as if Gilli's prayer had awakened a new and sharper awareness of him in Anna. She stood, lost, in the sumptuous sitting room while he quietly pulled the door to Gilli's room closed. Then he completely destroyed her with a casual touch, lightly sliding his hands over the knobs of her shoulders and down her arms about midway to the elbow. Those few inches of contact warmed, stunned and scared her. She felt fourteen again, craving his attention and understanding. She wanted him to like her, to approve of her, to love her.

Thank You for Anna 'cause You love her, too, and she's my goodest friend.

Anna knew intellectually that God loved everyone, but she had never *felt* loved. Why, she wondered, was that, and how pathetic was it that her "goodest" friend these days was a three-year-old child? On Sunday, Anna had dropped by the Elkanors' place with gifts, a small framed drawing and a bag of disposable diapers, for the new baby. She'd been gratified by the drawing's reception. The proud parents had both exclaimed over it and carefully examined every detail, but watching them with their baby, Anna had felt very much as if she were on the outside looking in, as usual.

Somehow, at this moment she felt even more isolated than

ever, isolated by a yearning for the impossible. Every moment at dinner she had been aware that she was not a true part of the family that gathered around the table, so she had done what she always did. She had teased and joked and showed off. She'd cast surreptitious glances at the man beside her like the lovesick fourteen-year-old she had once been and tried to read the answers to her hopes in every word and gesture.

She stood there in that lovely sitting room and admitted that her foolish heart had long ago set itself on something that could never be hers, and the pain of that suddenly threatened to overwhelm her. It was always best, Anna had found, to get as far away from disappointment as quickly as possible, but the instant she took a step through the door onto the broad central landing, Reeves spoke.

"I'll walk you down."

"Oh." She half turned. "You don't have to do that. I'm sure you're tired and—"

"I told Aunt Hypatia that I would see you out," he insisted, taking her by the arm.

Making a smile, Anna let him steer her along the landing to the top of the stairs. As they were descending the broad curving steps, he spoke again. "Can I ask you something?"

"You just did," she cracked.

He went on as if he hadn't even heard her. "Don't you miss going to church? Worship, I mean."

The question took her so off guard that she blurted the first thing that came into her head. "Why should I?"

He measured her with a sidelong glance. "How else do you expect to maintain a healthy relationship with God?"

In light of her recent thoughts, that rocked her back enough that she had to actually consider her answer. "There are other ways to maintain a healthy relationship with God."

"Such as?"

"Well, reading the Bible, praying."

"Do you? Regularly? Routinely?"

She tried, but invariably she let it slide or simply forgot. Too embarrassed to admit that, she said, "There are other ways to worship besides in church, you know. Haven't you ever praised God in a quiet meadow or forest glade?"

"Sure. Are you telling me that you take a nature hike every Sunday morning to worship God?"

Anna bowed her head. "No, of course not, but there's always the TV."

"Televised services are a godsend for shut-ins and others who can't travel to a church," he conceded, "but for everyone else just getting up and getting to church is an act of worship in obedience. Don't you think God values that?"

They reached the foot of the staircase before she had formulated a reply. It was an honest one; she couldn't seem to find another. "Yes, but in my case I wouldn't be worshiping. I'd be too aggravated by how much I had pleased my grandmother just by being there."

Reeves bowed his head, pondering that. "So," he said carefully, "she controls even your ability to worship God."

Anna almost dropped where she stood. She caught hold of the curved mahogany railing to steady herself, her heart pounding painfully as his conclusion sank in. The deep breath that she sucked in hurt almost as much as the truth.

"I've never understood you," he told her bluntly, not that it was anything she didn't already know. His puzzlement furrowed his brow, and she quelled the urge to brush back his streaky brown hair. "When my parents split, they actually broke up my home. It was so hard, trying to live in two different places. God knows I never wanted that for my own daughter. You, on the other hand, always lived with your wealthy grandmother, who seemed to give you everything you needed."

"Except approval," Anna said.

He stood there for several seconds, before murmuring, "So

you worked to earn her disapproval instead. And you still are."

That stung, sharply enough to make her retort, "Which is why I'm so concerned for Gilli."

His coppery eyes narrowed. "What do you mean?"

Determined to make him understand, she grasped his forearm with both hands. "In the beginning, rebellion may be just a way to get attention, but over time it can become…punishment for those who hurt o-or disappoint you. Worse, it gets to be a habit."

She could almost see him replaying things in his mind and would have given her next breath to know what they were. She desperately wanted to make him see, for Gilli. And for herself.

After several moments, he nodded. "I get it. Yes." To her absolute shock, he took her hands in his. "Thank you. Thank you for sharing that and for caring about my daughter," he said, his molten copper gaze holding hers. "Thank you especially for spending time with her. It's made a difference, all of it."

Several heartbeats ticked by before Anna realized that she was standing there with her jaw flapping in the breeze. Snapping her mouth shut, she managed a nod.

Reeves tucked one of her hands into the curve of his arm and stepped off across the foyer. Somehow, she kept pace with him, despite feeling a step behind.

"I just have one more question," he said companionably, drawing up in front of the yellow door. "How is that rebellion thing working for you nowadays?"

Bleakly, Anna realized what he was telling her, that she'd been stuck in that rut too long; yet, she couldn't imagine how to get out of it. Any softening on her part would be seen by Tansy as a tacit admission of defeat. But wasn't that the problem? This ongoing war of theirs had been at a stalemate for…how long now?

"Isn't it time," Reeves asked softly, "for you to start thinking about what is best for you instead of what makes your grandmother unhappy? They aren't always mutually exclusive, you know."

Anna blinked up at him. "When did you get so smart?" she whispered.

Reeves chuckled. "I could ask you the same thing. Taken us some time, though, hasn't it?" He sighed. "Maybe we're just a pair of slow learners, Anna." He shook his head, one corner of his mouth crooking up. "Better late than never, though, huh?"

She smiled. "That's what I hear."

His smile matching hers, he reached for her hand and squeezed it. For one heart-stopping moment their gazes held, and she actually thought, wondered, hoped… He leaned forward slightly—and pressed a kiss to her forehead before dropping her hand and stepping back.

"Drive safely."

"I—I will."

He opened the door, and she stumbled through it, her head reeling. "Good night."

"Good night."

He waited until she moved across the porch and down the steps to her car before closing the door behind her. Anna stood in the dark, staring up at the big, silent house. It was, perhaps, the loneliest moment of her life.

Chapter Eight

Reeves had given her much to think about, and Anna did not shirk the task, going over and over in her mind all that had been said between them and much that had not. The guilt came unexpectedly. For the first time, Anna realized that she had allowed her anger at her grandmother to keep her from doing much that she should have done, even from worshiping God. She had been so fixated on her resentment of Tansy and her treasured independence that she had blocked out everything else. Or did it go deeper than that? Had she been secretly angry with God all this time?

Surely, He could have seen to it that one of her parents had been around to love her and make her feel wanted. He could have made her life a heaven on earth, if He'd wanted to. Except there was no such thing. Heaven was heaven. This life was… problematic. She wondered why that was. Suddenly she wondered about so much and was shocked by how few answers she seemed to have, despite a childhood spent in church. She knew, admitted, that she needed to be in God's house, really be in God's house, on a regular basis, but oh, how the idea of pleasing Tansy chafed.

Feeling uncharacteristically tentative and pensive, she

went into work on Tuesday morning a bit late without even realizing it. Apparently, she was quieter than usual after the regular dressing down by Dennis, for Howard came to her corner to ask if she was okay.

"I'm fine. Didn't sleep much last night, that's all."

"I hear you. Sometimes, for no reason at all, you just can't shut it down."

She nodded, pondered, and said, "Howard, you and Lois go to church."

He stared at her for several moments through his too-large glasses. "That's right."

"Where exactly?"

He told her, then, "You looking for someplace to go, Anna?"

She sat there for a long time trying to nod, but finally she shook her head, knowing that she wouldn't go anywhere but to Downtown Bible. She wished that was not the case, but she knew that it was. Downtown Bible Church was home even if she hadn't attended a service there in years. "No, I just wondered."

He stood there for a moment longer, then her phone rang, and he walked away. She lifted the receiver and cradled it between her ear and shoulder.

"Print Shop. This is Anna. How can I help you?"

Hypatia Chatam spoke to her from the other end of the line, asking that she drop by that evening. "It's a minor thing, dear. We'll discuss it when you get here, say, half past five?"

"Sure."

"So good of you. We won't keep you long. Have a blessed day."

Anna hung up, wondering less what that was about than if she would see Reeves and Gilli. Just that she wondered made her queasy. She'd felt a slowly growing sense of unease since that moment after Gilli's prayer, and it was becoming more and more difficult to ignore.

Work became her cover. She crawled beneath it, buried herself with it, so that when the end of the day came she could only wonder where the time had gone. With equal parts dread and eagerness, she took her leave of Dennis and Harold and drove over to Chatam House.

Odelia came to the door wearing electric blue lace and stick people earrings, a pink female, a blue male. Anna looked at that little blue stickman and blurted out what was on her mind.

"Is Reeves here?"

She could've strangled herself.

"Not yet. He had to stop by his house for a word with his builder."

"Ah." Because she felt so deflated, Anna naturally acted pleased. "In that case, what can I do for you?"

"In here," Odelia directed, waving her toward the front parlor.

Anna followed and was soon going through a box of forms, one pad of which had a smudge in one portion of the design. "I don't know what that is," she said. "It could be something as simple as someone bumping into the printer during the process. Ink, unfortunately, smears. But it's not on any of the other pads. I'll replace this one and make sure it doesn't happen again."

"Oh, no, dear," Hypatia said, taking the offending pad from her hand. "It won't be necessary to replace this. We just wanted to call your attention to the matter in case it could become a larger problem."

"I don't think that's likely to happen."

"Ah. Just what we wanted to hear."

Anna smiled. Odelia asked how her day had gone.

"Oh, fine."

Unusually chatty, Magnolia wanted to know what she had actually done, explaining, "We find your work so fascinating."

Bemused, Anna gave her a brief overview of her day, if only to prove that nothing about it was fascinating. Hypatia offered her tea, which she declined, thinking it too close to the dinner hour. She noticed that Mags sent Odelia a troubled glance, but she didn't think too much about that. What went on in the minds of these triplets one never knew. Though they were dear old things, they were each a bit of a trip.

She got up to go, saying, "I'll see myself out."

They gave each other helpless looks, then smiled and nodded. Partly mystified and partly amused, Anna strode out into foyer.

A movement in the shadows in the back of the hallway snagged her attention. Peering closely, she spied Gilli sitting with her back against the wall, her chin propped atop her drawn-up knees.

"Hello, there, goodest friend," Anna ventured.

"'Lo."

Anna knew a sulk when she heard one. She ambled closer, studying the child who sat forlornly on the floor in the darkness of the shadows of dusk. "Something wrong?"

Gilli hitched up a shoulder in a shrug. Anna pinched the creases of her loose, olive-green slacks and slid down the wall to sit by the girl. She tugged her snug, cowl-necked ivory sweater into place and straightened the buckle of her wide brown belt, drawing up her knees so that the soles of her brown flats met the floor. Draping her forearms over her knees, she studied her companion.

"Want to tell me about it?"

Gilli shook her head. Anna tried another tack. Thinking of what Odelia had mentioned about Reeves meeting with his builder, she said, "I bet you'll be glad to get back home."

Gilli's knees dropped like rocks. Slinging her hands as if to rid them of something unpleasant, she cried, "I don't wanna go back there!"

Anna felt her brows leap upward. "No? Why not?"

"It's better *here,*" Gilli insisted, folding her arms.

Anna let that settle, considering things from Gilli's point of view. "More fun, I guess."

Gilli shrugged again, muttering, "I don't wanna go back and be by myself."

"But you won't be alone," Anna pointed out. "Your daddy will be there with you."

Gilli looked at her helplessly and began to cry. "I don't wanna go back there. A nanny will come and Daddy will go to work."

Anna slung an arm around her and hugged her to her side. "It's all right. Your daddy won't forget about you. He loves you."

Sniffing, Gilli asked in a trembling voice, "How you know?"

For a moment, Anna was too taken aback to speak, but then she tried to answer in a way Gilli would understand. "Why, it's obvious. He lives with you, doesn't he? Lots of daddies don't live with their kids, but he tucks you in at night and sees to it that you eat well and have pretty clothes. He teaches you to be polite and how to behave. He even prays with you and takes you to church. All in all, I'd say he's a wonderful father, a wonderful man, even. Why, I wanted a daddy just like him when I was a girl, a daddy who would take me home to live with him."

Gilli blinked at her, clearly shocked. "You didn't live with your daddy?"

Anna shook her head. "Nope. Not my daddy or my mommy. I had to live with my grandmother."

Gilli frowned, a troubled look on her face. Then she whispered, "My mommy went away."

Anna beat back the tears that sprang to her eyes and tightened her arm about the child. "Some mommies," she explained carefully, "do go away. It's very sad, I know, but let me tell you something, Gilli Leland. I feel sorry for your mommy because she doesn't get to see you every day. She doesn't know what a bright, fun, beautiful girl you are." She laid her check atop Gilli's curly head, whispering, "If I had a little girl, I'd want her to be just like you."

"Oh, there's just one Gilli," said a voice out of the darkness at the far end of the hall, startling them both.

"Daddy!"

Gilli sprang up and ran down the hall to meet him, giving Anna time to gather her composure and get to her own feet. "Hello, sugar," she heard him say.

For one wild moment, Anna considered making a dash for the door, but then she heard him walking toward her. He materialized out of the deep shadow at the end of the hall, carrying Gilli on his hip, his tan overcoat hanging open over his suit. Her arms about his neck, Gilli hugged him tightly.

"Anna," he said, his warm gaze sweeping over her.

"I—I didn't hear you come in."

"I know." He smiled at her. "You're looking very pretty today. I especially like the sweater."

She gurgled out a "Thank you," wondering just how long he'd been standing there in the shadows. She waved lamely toward the front door. "Gotta go."

"No," he said, "not yet. I need to speak to you. Just give me a minute."

Anna meekly followed at a distance as Reeves carried his daughter to the stairs.

"Come here," he said, standing her on the third step up from the floor. "I want to talk to you, too."

He sat down, and Gilli sat down next to him, hunching her shoulders. "Anna's right," he said, sweeping a hand over her adorable curls. "You are a bright, fun, beautiful little girl, and I'm sorry if I've let you be lonely sometimes. I didn't mean to. I hope you know that, because Anna's right about something else. I love you very much, and I'll never let you be lonely again, not ever."

Blinking back tears, Anna covered her mouth with her hand. Gilli launched herself up onto her knees and threw her arms around his neck, squeezing tightly.

"I love you bery mush, too, Daddy."

He laughed. Sort of. That was quite a chokehold she had on him. When she finally loosened her grip, he patted her and instructed, "Go tell our aunties that I'm home. Okay?"

"Yes, *please,*" she said, displaying her manners if not quite correctly.

Reeves pressed a finger to his lips, one hand holding her in place. "Excuse me," he said solemnly. "*Please* go tell the aunties that I'm home."

She popped up and bounced down the stairs, little legs pumping. "Okay! You're welcome!"

"Thank you," he said belatedly and shook his head, grinning. She disappeared into the drawing room, crying, "Daddy's home!"

Reeves sighed, but he didn't get up right away. Instead, he beckoned to Anna. She moved toward him tentatively. He held out his hand, and she placed her own in it, allowing him to pull her down to sit next to him. He started to speak to her, but then he bowed his head and began to pray.

"Thank You, Lord. I see You answering my prayers. Every day You draw me a little closer to You and to my daughter, to the Christian father and man I want to be. Thank You. Thank You so much." He sat for a moment longer, squeezing Anna's hand so tightly that her fingers ached. Finally, he looked up, tears sparkling in his eyes. "Thank you, Anna. What you said back there means more to me than you know." Then he slid his free hand into the hair at the back of her head and pulled her toward him, bringing her lips to his.

Stunned, Anna froze. Yet, somewhere in the back of her mind she was counting.

Thousand one, thousand two, thousand three, thousand four.

Those were perhaps the most wonderful four seconds of

her life, and then it was over. Suddenly she was staring into his copper eyes, her heart hammering with painful hope. Gratitude, she reminded herself, jumping to her feet. Just gratitude. Nothing more.

"Uh, go," she babbled. "I—I have to..." She gestured behind her.

He nodded, just once. Anna ran to grab her things from the table in the foyer, suddenly desperate to get out the door.

"Don't," she told herself, throwing on her coat and hurrying across the porch. "Don't think it. Don't dream it. Don't even want it."

But she did. Oh, she did.

Dennis printed the invitations to the gala auction on Monday morning. Anna examined each one by hand and found them perfect. She even crosschecked every name and address on the accompanying envelopes against the voluminous mailing list. All that remained was for the envelopes to be stuffed and dropped into the mail.

When Anna called to set a time for the delivery, she was a bit surprised to be told once again to come at the end of the day. She had expected to conduct an immediate transport, given the eagerness of the Chatam sisters to get their hands on the invitations. They had called several times during the past week to check on the progress, and she couldn't blame them for being anxious. March had arrived the day before, not that the weather had changed one iota. It was, however, that much closer to the date of the fund-raiser.

Intending to drop off the invitations and go, Anna stood shivering inside her cowboy boots, leggings and oversize, dark red sweater on the veranda of Chatam House at precisely five o'clock that afternoon. She rang the bell with her elbow, the box of invitations secure in her arms, her keys dangling from her teeth. The keys hit the deck when Reeves opened that yellow door.

She truly had not expected to see him, had counted on not doing so, in fact. Given what had happened between them the last time they'd met, she had figured he would be as wary of seeing her again as she was of meeting up with him. Yet, there he stood wearing a huge grin, along with comfortable jeans, athletic shoes and a long-sleeved rusty orange T-shirt.

"Oops," he said. Bending, he swept up the keys and backed out of the doorway so she could enter. "Trade you," he said, reaching for the box.

She pocketed the keys somewhat warily. "I didn't expect to see you here."

"I'm trying to cut back on my hours a bit, spend a little more time with Gilli."

"Ah. She must be pleased."

"Not pleased enough to miss a fast-food dinner and playdate, I'm afraid. She's with my stepmother and baby sister. My father had a business dinner, so it seemed like a good time to get the girls together. I'm just the drop-off and pickup service today."

"That's all right," Anna told him. "At least you're here to do it. That's what matters, believe me."

The sharp planes of his face softened. "I believe you."

Suddenly her heartbeat doubled. Good sense told her that it was stupid to be here yearning for what she'd already accepted would never be hers. She should go. She'd done her job and done it well. The invitations had been delivered; she knew they were perfect, so the Chatams could have no complaint. No one in her right mind would keep opening the same wormy can, but here she was, just as helplessly dim-witted as she'd been way back at the beginning of high school. Lest she doubt it, when Reeves beckoned, she followed him.

He spoke to her over his shoulder as he led the way, not into the parlor but down the hallway to the right of the sweeping staircase, where she had never ventured. "The aunties are cracking the whip in the ballroom. They've set up something of a production line. I suspect they'll have these in the mail within the hour."

They walked past a sumptuously appointed library that would have made many small towns envious before they came to a small, closed door.

"What's in there?" she asked, her curiosity temporarily overriding everything else.

"Music room," he told her, walking on toward the nearest of two sets of broad pocket doors. "Sections of one wall slide apart so that it opens into the ballroom."

Music rooms, cloakrooms, ballrooms… Despite the number of times she'd been in this house, it was hard to believe anyone lived this way. She suddenly felt as if she'd fallen down the rabbit hole.

Reeves turned right and disappeared. Anna followed, coming to an abrupt halt as the cavernous space beyond those pocket doors revealed itself. That rabbit hole turned out not to be far off the mark. It was like something right out of a fairy tale: marble and gilt and burnished oak with ceiling-to-floor windows draped in muted blue and yellow, crystal and a coffered ceiling overhead. Anna stared, unabashedly taking in every detail, while Reeves carried the box to a table set up at the near end of the room.

The exclamations of the aunties, as Reeves called them, and their "production line" pulled Anna's attention back to the matter at hand.

"Oh, Anna Miranda, they're wonderful!" Odelia gushed, hurrying across the floor to hug her. Fortunately, given the older woman's penchant for big jewelry, fur dangled from her earlobes, big balls of white fluff that perfectly matched the cuffs and collar of her purple-and-white windowpane-check dress, not to mention the pompoms on her shoes, which looked suspiciously like white bedroom slippers. Anna grinned with delight.

"I'm so glad you're pleased."

Odelia linked arms with her and towed her across the room, where Hypatia was calling her babbling troops to order.

"Ladies, ladies. Your attention, please." Her hands folded at her waist, Hypatia announced importantly, "Our graphic designer, Anna Burdett."

A wave of delicate applause followed. Anna knew all but a couple of the faces around that table. She was surprised but relieved not to see her grandmother's among them, even as she did the polite thing.

"Thank you. That's very kind but not at all necessary."

"It definitely is," Reeves refuted, examining one of the invitations that the ladies were now eagerly removing from the box. "You've captured the spirit of the thing exactly, an excellent job."

Anna was so nonplussed by his praise that she didn't even manage a thank-you this time.

Hypatia waved a hand dismissively, ordering, "Now run along, the two of you. We have work to do."

Winking, Reeves caught Anna's hand in his, and she found herself once again being towed across that marble floor.

"I have something for you," he told her, "something I think you'll find interesting. I didn't know what to do with it, at first. Then I hit on the idea of a database."

Puzzled, Anna allowed herself to be swept back along the hall and into the library.

"Sit," he directed, waving toward a pair of black leather armchairs positioned at slight angles to a most unusual rectangular table. Atop it lay an orange binder. "Relax," he invited, moving to an oddly shaped cabinet standing against one wall. "Get comfortable."

Anna did neither. She was too busy wondering how he could behave so casually. Didn't he remember that he'd kissed her? To cover her agitation, she ran her hand over the glossy, coppery wood.

"I've never seen a table like this. What is it?" she asked, examining the unique diamond-shaped marquetry on the side and legs.

Reeves glanced back over his shoulder. "It's a Henredon. We know that because it's signed underneath. I believe the style is called Chinese Chippendale."

Anna fought the urge to drop to all fours to check out that signature, not that she had any idea who Henredon might be. "What kind of wood?"

"Light red mahogany, I believe. Grandpa Hub was especially proud of that piece."

"I can imagine."

"What'll you have?" he asked, opening the upper doors of the cabinet to reveal a beverage bar, complete with a small sink, a row of empty crystal decanters and a silver ice bucket, along with various sodas, bottled water, a box of powdered drinks and an electric teapot. "We've got tea, coffee, tea, apple cider, tea, cocoa and, of course, tea." Tossing her a grin, he opened a lower door and took out a mug. "I'm going for the cider myself." She watched him tear open a packet, dump the contents into the mug and pour in hot water. "There's ice if you'd prefer a cold drink."

"Uh." She waved a hand. "Whatever. So long as it's hot."

"Okay, cider it is."

He went through the process again, stirred both cups and carried them to the table. She winced when he set the steaming drinks on that lovely wood. He folded down into the chair facing hers, picked up one of the mugs and sat back to sip.

"Mmm, not bad."

He looked at her over the rim of his mug, and Anna's every nerve ending quivered. She snatched up the other mug and stuck her nose in it.

"Very nice. Uh, you…you said something about a database?"

"Mmm." Leaning forward, he set aside the mug and reached for the binder on the table. "I ran across some interesting info recently, and I thought you might like to see it."

"Info," she parroted uncertainly.

"About the many applications of your particular expertise."

"Expertise?" She shook her head, feeling particularly idiotic. "I don't understand."

He laid the folder in her lap, picked up his mug and leaned back. "I was surprised, frankly, by how many industries and processes require graphic artists. Many are work-from-home positions."

Anna stared at him uncomprehendingly for long seconds, until he dropped his gaze, saying tentatively, "You seem unhappy with your current employment. I thought this might help."

It hit her then, like a sledgehammer to the back of the skull. He'd put this together, or had it put together, because of what she'd said about Dennis and her job. She got her mug back onto the table without spilling her drink and opened the binder.

Page after page after page of job descriptions, business perspectives, Web site addresses, even names and contacts, all for graphic artists. All for her. Something lurched and stretched inside of her, like a sleeper awakened from a long, unknowing slumber. It thrilled and terrified her all at the same time.

"Why?" was the only thing she could think to say.

"To thank you," Reeves said, sounding earnest and fond. "You've been so kind to Gilli and the aunties. I know they can be demanding, time-consuming and—"

"No! Oh, no," she cut in. "Gilli's a delight, and your aunts, well, they've been utterly charming to work with."

He smiled knowingly. "Charming is their stock-in-trade, as I'm sure you know. It's how they get exactly what they want."

"And you obviously learned at their knees," she muttered, thinking better of it only when it was too late. As usual.

He opened his mouth as if to reply but then said not a word. Quickly she tucked the binder beneath her arm and rose, her cheeks heating. How blatant could she be, for pity's sake?

"It's very thoughtful of you to, er, think of me." She edged away from the chair, babbling, "Sorry I have to run. Tell Gilli…" Her brain stuttering, she pasted on a fatuous smile and finished lamely with, "You know. And, um… Bye."

He was still sitting there impersonating a cod when she turned her back and all but ran, that binder clutched to her chest. She knew that she was going to treasure the silly thing for the rest of her days simply because he had put it together for her.

"To thank you," he'd said. For being kind, no less. For failing to live up to his worst expectations of the brat, more like.

Yes, she would treasure the folder and the effort that it represented, but that was it. Period. End of story. End of dream. End of foolishness. Gratitude, however well meant, would never be enough for her, and that's all she could ever realistically expect from him. So this, then, was also the end of hope.

It was better that way, she decided, for hope invariably brought the pain of disappointment.

Chapter Nine

Charm! Reeves stared into the mug of cooling cider and looked for some element of truth in the undissolved powder that settled on the bottom of the cup. They must have different definitions of the term. First, he'd given her a hard time, followed by a meaningless box of chocolates and a thank-you card, for Valentine's, no less. Then he'd given her a database of job prospects and a cup of powdered apple cider.

Yeah, he was smooth, all right.

Marissa had not found him charming, at least not once they'd wed. She had called him dull and cold and unimaginative, while explaining that she needed a "real" man to make her feel like a woman.

What did Anna need? he wondered. What did Anna want? He was pretty sure about one thing. She did not seem to look at his Chatam connections and see dollar signs.

He suspected that was the only reason Marissa had married him. She had been so disappointed to realize that he would likely never see a nickel of the Chatam millions. He suspected that his own mother had blown her inheritance ages ago, and even if she had not, he had three siblings in direct line for that money. As for the aunties, so far they had five nephews, seven nieces and seven greats of one gender or the other. He would be foolish in the extreme to count on inheriting anything from them. Why should he? He made a good living, but that hadn't been enough for Marissa.

He sat there shaking his head and listening to the grandfather clock in the corner tick off the seconds until it was time to go after Gilli. Rising, he carried both barely touched mugs to the sink. Without a word to anyone, he got his brown leather jacket and went out to his car.

Little more than fifteen minutes later, he walked through the fast-food restaurant toward the indoor playground. He opened the glass door that segregated the children's space from a restaurant full of strangers and walked into earsplitting chaos. Surveying the crowd of parents and children for his daughter, he spied instead the long auburn hair of his stepmother, Layla, his father's third wife.

All of five years his senior, Layla had been his father's legal secretary and was now the mother of his nearly four-year-old baby sister Myra, whom Reeves saw next. Myra wore a pink-and-white polka-dot bow in the sleek auburn hair that she had inherited from her mother. Her knit pantsuit matched the bow, as did the bows on her black Mary Janes. She looked like she'd just stepped out of a picture book. Beside her, in head-to-toe maroon suede, Layla just looked angry. It was only when Layla shook her finger in Gilli's face that he finally found his daughter.

Gilli was sobbing. Her curly hair stuck out in a dozen places, as if she'd been pulled headfirst through the towering maze of crawling tubes. Bedraggled and dirty, she looked like a street urchin next to Myra. Sighing, Reeves made his way through the churning bodies and din to their table, arriving in time to hear Layla yell, "Never again!"

"Never again what?" he asked loudly.

Layla turned on him, her otherwise attractive face twisted into a disapproving mask. She thrust a perfectly manicured finger at Gilli. "That child is incorrigible! She attacked Myra!"

Gilli wailed even louder. Standing there in the midst of the madness, Reeves felt as if his head would explode, but for once he was going to give Gilli the benefit of the doubt. Seizing each of the girls by a hand, he turned and hauled them through the crowd and out the door, leaving Layla to gather their things and follow as she saw fit. The instant the din of the playroom dimmed behind them, Gilli's sobs waned, too. She was mostly gasping and shuddering by the time he found a quiet corner booth and parked her and Myra on opposite sides of it.

"What's this about?" he asked as Layla came huffing up behind him. He went down on his haunches, keeping his voice low. "Gilli, I want you to tell me why you hit Myra."

Gilli's head came up, and she wailed, "Myra pull my hair!"

Reeves turned to his baby sister, whose chin now rested on her chest, and asked, "Myra, why did you pull Gilli's hair?"

Myra looked up, her dark eyes sparkling with tears. After a moment, she whispered, "Gilli wins. Ever time we race, she always wins."

Reeves knew instantly what had happened. They were racing around the climbing structure to see who could get on the ladder next, and Gilli had been in the lead. "Did you grab her hair on purpose?" To her credit, Myra nodded glumly. "So you yanked her hair and Gilli punched you in retaliation," he clarified, making sure Layla heard every word.

"I didn't see that," Layla said crisply. "I just saw Gilli hit Myra."

Reeves heart wrung. How many times had he just assumed that Gilli was the lone culprit? He cleared his throat and calmly went on.

"So you're both to blame, which means that you have something to say to each other, doesn't it?"

Myra sank a little lower on the bench before muttering, "I'm sorry I pulled your hair, Gilli."

Gilli straightened and wiped at her glimmering eyes, leaving dirty smears on her face. "Sorry, too."

"All right," Reeves said, smiling, "I think we're done here. Time to go."

He twisted up and out of the booth, reaching for Gilli's coat. As she slid to the floor, he shook out the coat then began helping her into it. Gilli looked up at him, gratitude shining in her eyes, and her little hand crept into his. Pride swelled in him.

Turning to his stepmother, he quietly said, "Next time, get the full story." She nodded curtly, her gaze averted. "Say goodbye, girls," he instructed.

They exchanged waves and overly cheery "byes."

Reeves squeezed Gilli's hand, and together they walked out to the car. As he was lifting her into her seat, he thought he ought to clarify a few things while he was still in her good graces.

"Gilli," he said, "no matter what someone else does to you, it's not okay to hit or pull hair. You know that, don't you?"

"Yes, Daddy."

"I expect you and Myra to behave better next time. Understand?"

"Yes, Daddy."

"Good. Let's get you buckled in."

"No!"

Shocked by her sudden vehemence, he opened his mouth to scold, but she threw her arms around his neck and squeezed tight, whispering, "Love you, Daddy."

Gulping, he wrapped his long arms around her. "I love you, too, sugar." Drawing back, he cupped her face in his big hands and studied it. What he saw took his breath away. "You're a happier girl now, aren't you, my Gilli?"

She nodded. He wasn't sure she really understood the

question, but she was eager to give him whatever answer he wanted, and that was more than answer enough.

"I'm a happier daddy, too," he told her, bending to kiss her forehead.

She grinned just as if she knew that she was the reason, and of course she was, but it wasn't just her.

He knew who got the credit for this unexpected turn of events. First, God Almighty, Who had commanded the honeybees to drive them out of their house, and second, the aunties with their calm, charming, interfering faith and the warm sanctuary of Chatam House. And finally, Anna.

So much for which to be thankful. So many reasons to praise his Lord.

"Sweet Jesus," he whispered, standing beside his car there in the cold parking lot, his happy child safely buckled inside. "Sweet, sweet Jesus. Thank You."

His soul brimming with praise, he couldn't think of any other words to say until they fell out of his mouth.

"Let there be a happier Anna, too."

Anna had never felt so hopeless. She didn't know why. Nothing had changed. She'd never believed, not even as a fourteen-year-old with a killer crush, that she could have the sort of life that everyone else seemed to. In all honesty, she'd never found much to like about herself, and that probably would not be any different if her parents had lived. The only thing she found to value was her independence, however tenuous. As a whole, she was a disappointment, barely able to pay her bills, hold her controlling grandmother at bay—or form a private, more personal relationship.

In truth, she'd never imagined herself romantically involved with anyone except Reeves, but he remained as unattainable as ever. A successful, stalwart Christian like Reeves Leland could never have any genuine personal interest in her. Gilli liked her, and he felt grateful to her, but that was all it amounted to, all it *could* amount to. Anna could do nothing about that, but she could do something about her relationship with God.

She kept hearing Reeves ask when she had last worshipped. God deserved worship. She had forgotten that in her battle for independence from her grandmother. What God must think of her! No doubt, she was as much a disappointment to Him as everyone else, so she got down on her knees and confessed. With tears rolling down her face, she apologized to God for failing to worship Him, for allowing her resentments and stubbornness to keep her from giving Him His due. Then she made up her mind to do better.

It wasn't easy. She already knew that she couldn't, was not supposed to, go anywhere but to the Downtown Bible Church. That meant facing not only her grandmother but Reeves and the Chatam sisters, everyone who had wondered why she was not in church and everyone who had invited her to join them over the years. So many had made polite inquiries and invitations, and she had blown off every one of them without a qualm. It seemed fitting then that she do this alone.

She rose early on Sunday morning and donned, ugh, pantyhose and a long-sleeved mauve shift belted at the waist with four-inch-wide purple suede leather perfectly matched to the only pair of heels that she owned. Despite taking pains with her appearance, she arrived early in the arched foyer of the sanctuary. She walked alone across an expanse of dark gold carpet to the tall, arched double door with its heavy black wrought iron hardware. Inside the sanctuary, a full dozen chandeliers hanging high overhead echoed the black wrought iron theme. They, along with their heavy, draping chains, added a Southwest flavor to the stately interior.

Little had changed in the years since Anna had last been here, but the few changes were startling. As always, milk-white, plastered walls stood punctuated by tall, elaborate, stained glass windows and soaring beamed arches leading to sumptuous gold leaf high overhead. Familiar, pale polished wood lay underfoot, softened now by strategically placed runners of gold carpet. Row upon row of long pews, now padded in startling turquoise velvet, still led to the massive altar and the railed apse with its raised, carpeted platform, throne-like chairs and pulpit. The glass baptistery at the very front stood flanked by the golden pipes of an ancient organ, the console of which was hidden in the loft positioned above the foyer, but two large video screens had been added, one high on either side and just in front of the apse. Both sat at an angle that did not distract from the dramatic tableau below. Neither did the railed spaces on either side of the wide aisle before the altar where a full orchestra and choir were already beginning to gather.

Anna had forgotten how much she loved this grand space, how it quieted the soul and set the mind on God and His glories. Walking swiftly to the far end of the nearest pew, she sat down closest to the wall and bowed her head, hoping that her grandmother would not venture in before the spaces around her filled with enough people to provide her with camouflage. As she sat there, stillness filled her. Even her troubled thoughts dissolved, and she felt her breaths come and go with peaceful ease.

After some time, the organ began to play, the music softly soaring and rippling. Soon the buzz of people finding their seats and greeting their brethren overlay the music, but Anna kept her head down. The pew rocked slightly as someone else dropped down onto it, and a shoulder bumped hers.

"Well, well, just who I most wanted to see here."

A thrill of satisfaction shot through her, but she tamped it down before tilting her head. Reeves grinned at her, and she suddenly felt terribly conspicuous. Glancing around the now bustling room, she lifted a hand to the fringe of hair at her nape, telling herself that his delight stemmed from nothing more than Christian concern.

To cover both her discomfort and her pleasure, she asked, "Where's Gilli?"

Crossing his legs, Reeves pinched the crease in the cuff covering the ankle that he balanced atop the opposite knee. "On her way to Children's Church."

Anna smiled. "No fuss?"

"None at all. Pardon me if I brag, but she's been a perfect delight lately." He grinned again, and goodness, was he attractive like this. "That is, if you don't mind having stray cats and dirt dragged into the house."

Anna's eyes went wide as she imagined what must have happened. "Oh, no."

He chuckled. "Yep, she finally caught that skinny gray cat that *you* knocked out of the tree that day. Poor Hypatia." Reeves sighed gustily, stretching an arm along the back of the pew behind her. "The sweet old dear is exercising a great deal of patience with us, I'm afraid."

Anna could just imagine Hypatia's reaction…all those priceless antiques and spotless floors. "You didn't blame me, did you?"

Reeves turned a face of purest innocence to her. "Of course, I did."

"Reeves!"

Laughing, he moved his arm to her shoulders and curled it tight. "I'm nobody's fool, sweetheart. They adore you, and I'm using that for all it's worth."

What protest could she make to such a pronouncement? Provided, that was, she could have gotten a word past the sudden constriction of her throat. Sweetheart. He had called her sweetheart.

Meaningless, she told herself. *Utterly meaningless.* Goofball would have served as well. She wished he'd called her that, anything that didn't make her wonder if he might actually *like* her. Good grief, was this going to be high school all over again?

At the front of the sanctuary, a man moved to a microphone and lifted a hand. The organ music stopped, and the man began welcoming one and all before calling their attention to the announcements now slowly scrolling across the video screens. The organ began to play again, very softly this time, and stillness once more settled over the room.

A woman stepped up to the microphone and asked the congregation to prepare themselves for worship. Reeves removed his arm from about Anna's shoulders and leaned forward, bowing his head. Surprised that he didn't rise and slip out to join his aunts or friends, she quickly followed suit. Closing her eyes, she reached for some sense of God in this place. And found it. When the formal call to worship came, spoken in reverent tones by the woman at the microphone, Anna was in silent prayer.

Dear Lord, I'm here, just as I promised, but please don't let my grandmother make a scene, and please don't let me embarrass myself. Most of all, please don't let me get all caught up in Reeves again when I know that could never work out. Amen.

The orchestra joined the organ, and the choir began a beautiful song based on Psalm 118. The congregation rose and joined in on the next selection. No hymnals. Instead, the words were projected onto the video screens. This was not a familiar hymn to Anna, and she felt lost. Beside her Reeves sang in a low, quiet bass, competent but with perhaps a limited range. She rather liked that tiny flaw in him. Later songs proved more familiar, but by that time Anna was content to simply let the music flow around her. She had forgotten, if she'd ever known, how sacred music could lift the spirit.

When the pastor stepped up into the pulpit, Anna tried not to regret the end of the music portion of the service. He began with a few joking remarks, but then he got down to business with a Scripture reading. The passage, Romans 8:1-8, flashed up onto the video screens, but Anna noticed that Reeves followed along in his Bible. She divided her attention between him and the video screen, until the sixth verse smacked her right between the eyes.

"The mind of sinful man is death," the pastor read, "but the mind controlled by the Spirit is life and peace."

Life and peace, Anna thought, staring at those words on the screen. Suddenly she knew that she desperately needed that. For years now, she'd been existing in some kind of solitary limbo, and in all that time she could not recall more than mere moments of peace. The satisfaction that she occasionally derived from displeasing her grandmother in no way offset the long, lonely days and nights, the emptiness and grief that she felt every time she thought of her parents, the uncertainty of her job, not to mention the general hopelessness of her life. Was that all she had to look forward to? Irritating Tansy, wondering about her parents, dragging herself into the shop every day and back to her dreary apartment again in the evening, alone? That did not seem like life to her. It certainly was not peace.

While she listened to the pastor, she watched Reeves make notes on a slip of paper that he'd drawn from inside the cover of his Bible. At one point, he underlined something in the Bible itself, and she wondered what it was in that passage that could apply to him. Looking back up to the screen, she decided that it must be the first verse.

Therefore, there is now no condemnation for those who are in Christ Jesus.

She had always known, never doubted, that Reeves was a Christian. Certainly, he did not live "according to the sinful nature." Somehow, even when he most irritated her and was most irritated by her, she had always realized that he lived by an inviolate code of conduct that she could only admire.

After a brief invitation, during which the pastor and others prayed with several individuals who came forward, the service moved toward a close. Anna snagged her handbag from the floor where she'd placed it earlier, nodded silently at Reeves and slipped out of the pew to hurry through those double doors—only to find Tansy waiting for her in the foyer.

"I can't believe my eyes!" her grandmother exclaimed, rushing toward her. "Why didn't you tell me you were going to be here?"

Anna made for the nearest exit, replying with her customary bluntness, "Because I didn't want you to know."

Tansy stepped in front of her. "Just tell me what's brought this about?"

"You wouldn't understand," Anna said, attempting to move around her. Tansy made an ungainly sideways hop to block her, and Anna panicked, looking around blindly for an escape. A long, square-palmed hand closed around her forearm.

"This way," Reeves said. Anna stared at him in confusion. "Children's Church," he went on, watching Tansy, "it's this way. Better hurry if we want to beat the crowd."

Gratefully, Anna followed, rushing to keep up as his long legs led her away from Tansy and through a doorway across the foyer into a hall. They were well out of sight when he turned into yet another long hallway. She finally drew up. Her feet, in shoes meant for nothing more demanding than a short, sedate saunter, were killing her. Reeves stopped and strolled back to where she slumped against the wall.

"Thank you."

He shrugged. "I assumed you didn't want a scene."

"You're right. I don't."

He lifted an eyebrow at that. "I can remember a time when you'd have relished one, done your best to embarrass Tansy."

Anna smiled wanly. "So can I."

He tilted his head. "Looks like the brat's grown up, after all. And yet, I suspect you're about to make a liar out of me."

"What do you mean?"

"I implied that we have plans."

"Which we don't."

"Not if you refuse to join us for Sunday dinner," he conceded pointedly. Anna blinked at him. "Mind you, the aunties eat 'simple' on Sundays," he hastened to add, "simple but ample. I'm sure they'd be delighted for you to join us. I know Gilli would."

Anna noticed that he didn't say anything about himself, but then she didn't expect him to. Why then was she disappointed?

"Let me add a little more incentive," he went on, stepping closer. "I doubt Tansy would follow you to Chatam House."

Anna widened her eyes in horror. "But she would trail me back to my place." Smiling, she quipped, "You sure know how to convince a girl, Stick."

"Charm," he said with a wink. "I learned it at the knees of my aunties, you know."

Anna shook her head. Not only had he rescued her from an ugly public scene, he'd found the perfect way to diminish her embarrassing gaffe of the day before. Always one to value a good joke, she retorted, "Baloney. It's genetic, bred into your very bones."

"Like the cleft chin."

They both laughed, and then he asked in an entirely conversational tone, "Where is your place anyway? I don't think I even know where you live."

"Cherry Hill Apartments."

"Ah, yes. The complex in that low spot out there by the highway."

She snickered. "That's right. The one with no cherry trees."

"Hmm, I'd have thought you were more the Peach Orchard type," he said, naming another apartment complex in town.

She shook her head with mock sincerity. "I don't particularly care for peaches."

"You mean they actually *have* peaches?"

"Of course not, but still…" She wrinkled her nose. "It's the principle of the thing."

"Right." His lips twitched.

"I did consider Pecan Valley," she said, just to keep the joke going.

"But?" he asked.

"They actually have pecan trees."

He arched both eyebrows. "How trite."

They laughed again.

Anna thought, *Look at us. We're having fun together!*

Who would ever have believed it? The Brat and the old Stick-in-the-Mud actually enjoying each other's company. It was, she suspected, as close to having her dreams come true as she would ever get.

Chapter Ten

"See!" Gilli ran into the parlor and came to an abrupt halt directly in front of Anna. "Here she is!"

Anna bit her lips. The skinny gray-on-gray striped cat hung by the neck from the crook of Gilli's arm, its also-gray eyes staring off into space. Anna would have thought it was paralyzed or traumatized if not for the lazy curl of the tip of its tail.

"He," Reeves corrected, leaning against the doorjamb. He had removed his coat and tie and rolled back the cuffs of his shirtsleeves. "Here *he* is."

Gilli nodded and announced, "Her name's Special."

"*His* name is Special."

"Uh-huh," Gilli agreed, petting the cat's narrow head. "Do you like her collar?"

Anna looked to Reeves, waiting for his correction. He shrugged and shook his head as if to say that it was pointless. Anna cleared her throat, looked at Gilli and commented, "It's, um, pink."

"Special likes pink!" Gilli declared. "Don't you, sweetie cat goodie dear?" She peppered her endearments with kisses to the cat's ears. Other than a single twitch, the cat might have been a stuffed toy.

Hypatia showed up in the doorway beside Reeves. She sent an exasperated look at Gilli, shoulders slumping.

"Gilli dear, what are you doing with that cat *now?* Luncheon is on the table. Come along. Reeves, see Anna into the dining room, will you?"

"With pleasure," he said, straightening away from the doorframe. He strolled toward Anna just as Hypatia swept Gilli and the cat from the room.

"Poor Hypatia," he remarked, "overcome by a three-year-old."

"And a cat named Special," Anna added, grinning.

"I suggested we name him Catatonic, but only the vet thought that was funny."

Anna sputtered laughter.

"You laugh," Reeves said, eyes sparkling, "but I spent a minor fortune on that critter before the veterinarian could convince Hypatia that it would make a safe house pet, although the jury's still out on its mental health."

"I adopted a baby possum once," Anna told him, still sputtering.

Reeves grinned. "Tansy must have loved that."

"She didn't know. Until it escaped. Silly thing fainted every time I got near it, or pretended to, then one day it bit me and ran."

He shook his head, still grinning. "Don't think that's going to happen in this case."

She lifted her eyebrows. "How can you say that?"

As if on cue, a high, plaintive "*mmmmrrrrroooowwww*" began to echo through Chatam House. Reeves crooked a finger at her. "You'll see."

Curious, she accompanied him to the dining room, where Hypatia sat with her head in her hands. Gilli occupied her usual chair, her feet swinging merrily as she spoke to a pet carrier on the seat next to her.

"There, there, Special baby doll dear. I right here."

Anna went to peer into the carrier. The cat was laid out on its side, as stiff as a corpse, the only sign of life that eerie, mournful, ceaseless howl that emanated from its open mouth. Alarmed, she looked to Reeves.

"What's wrong with it?"

"Gilli's not touching it, that's what's wrong with it," Reeves said.

"I will not have an animal loose at the table," Hypatia insisted.

Magnolia and Odelia entered through the butler's pantry then, carrying a loaf of bread and a pitcher of water, respectively.

"It's not working, Hypatia," Magnolia asserted, plunking the bread platter onto the table. Odelia placed the pitcher on the sideboard and cupped her hands around the twin fruit salads clipped to her earlobes.

"Oh, all right!" Hypatia snapped. "Anything to placate that absurd—" She cast a long-suffering look at Gilli. "Special." She sighed. "Anything for Special."

Magnolia promptly marched around the table, took the furry siren from its carrier, and draped it over a delighted Gilli's lap. The yowl abruptly faded to a purr. Gilli giggled and beamed.

While Magnolia went to rinse her hands, Reeves shook out his daughter's napkin and spread it over the now contented and apparently paralyzed cat, his gaze finding Anna's. She shook her head, amazed, but wisely kept her tongue glued to the floor of her mouth. Reeves came to escort her around the table to a chair, pulling it out for her and holding it until she smiled up at him. He went to seat his aunts before returning to take the chair at Anna's side.

Hypatia scowled and looked to Reeves. "Perhaps you would say the blessing?"

"Of course." He cleared his throat, and they all bowed their heads. "Most gracious Lord God, we thank You and we praise

You for this, Thy bounty, given for the nourishment of our bodies. Most of all, Father, I thank You for each woman around this table, child and adult alike, given, no doubt, for the nourishment of my heart. In the name of Christ Jesus, amen."

Anna quivered inside. Had he purposefully included her in his prayer of thanksgiving? For the nourishment of his heart? As if. What was he going to say, thanks for everyone but Anna?

Gilli patted the cat under the napkin on her lap, crooning, "You, too, sweetie Special girl."

Anna thought it as likely that the cat was included in Reeves prayer as her. Oh, no, wait. It was a male.

"Gilli," Reeves said, as if reading Anna's thoughts, "that cat really is a boy."

"I know." Gilli hunched her shoulders and crooned, "My beautiful boy sweetie."

Reeves rolled his eyes. Anna covered her mouth. Hypatia looked like she might weep. Magnolia and Odelia, on the other hand, seemed content to dish out soup and pass around the salad. Reeves and Anna shared a smile, then set to enjoying their own lunch.

The meal passed in near silence, as if the purr of the comatose cat draped over Gilli's lap blocked all conversation. It was perhaps the most physically uncomfortable hour of Anna's life. She hadn't worn this dress since the wedding for which she'd bought it, over two years ago, and she had forgotten how the belt cut grooves in the tops of her hips, the stockings itched like steel wool and the heels of her shoes made her feet swell. Plus, if there existed in this world a dish she disliked more than split pea soup, she hadn't tasted it.

Yet, somehow, she'd never been happier. Or sadder.

After lunch, Anna offered to help clean up, but Reeves could have told her that the aunties would have none of it.

They practically chased Reeves, Anna and Gilli from the dining room, along with the cat, of course. He suspected, from the knowing smile that Mags and Od shared, that they were indulging in a bit of matchmaking again, but he let it go. To his surprise, he enjoyed spending time with Anna, and he'd been thinking a lot about that kiss on the stairwell.

As much as he'd tried to tell himself that it had been an impulsive expression of gratitude, he knew better. Oh, it had been impulsive, all right, and gratitude was part of it, but that kiss had been as much about him as her. He didn't want to be alone. He had never wanted to be alone, and in the deepest well of his soul, he believed that God intended him to marry, despite the mistake he had made with Marissa. If the very idea of a "him and Anna" still boggled his mind, well, at least it was a more open and informed mind than it had been.

He suggested to her that they move to the library in hopes of discussing the dossier of information that he'd given her the last time they'd been there. He truly wanted Anna to be happy, but the most he could do was encourage her to look for another job. Before he could bring up the subject, however, Gilli seized upon the opportunity for a story. Anna took down a picture book, not a child's book but a nature book of desert photos, finding a surprising picture of a lizard, snake and hare in close proximity. Soon she and Gilli, a purring Special draped over one arm, had spun a fascinating tale of animals that cooperated to find water and shelter from the sun.

Afterward, Gilli screwed up her face and asked, "What is berrow?"

"Burrow," Anna corrected, reaching for a paper and pen that someone had left on the library table earlier. Quickly, she sketched a picture of a lizard squeezing into a snake's burrow, explaining as she drew.

"O-o-oh," Gilli said. Then she wrinkled her nose. "I wouldn't want to live in the dirt. And not in the bush, either.

That's where Special had to live, isn't it, dear baby sugar?" She stroked the cat as she spoke.

While listening to the story then watching Anna sketch, an idea had come to Reeves, one he wanted to explore with Anna, but just then Gilli yawned and duty called.

"Someone needs a nap."

Gilli immediately put up a howl. He just shook his head at her pleas.

"Can I help tuck you in again?" Anna asked, and that did it.

"Okay," Gilli conceded glumly.

They all went out and climbed the stairs together. Gilli carried the cat in a chokehold, but Reeves had learned from experience not to tamper with the arrangement. Whenever anyone tried to help her find a seemingly gentler way to handle it, the ridiculous animal hissed and showed its fangs. Reeves had no doubt that it would take off a finger if it sensed that anyone meant to truly separate it from Gilli. Besides, after showing her what would hurt the cat, the vet had said that the animal would teach them how it wanted to be handled. So far, the cat wanted to be handled only by Gilli, and obviously, no matter how awkward it looked, she wasn't hurting the silly thing. To her, the cat was a person, the dearest and sweetest of all beings, and she was wounded by anyone who suggested otherwise. She spoke to the animal as if she expected it to reply.

"We got to take a nap. Daddy says the world is better from a nap, but I think it's good without it. Don't you? Hmm?"

Despite hiding many a grin, they made short work of tucking in Gilli and her cat, which curled up next to her on her pillow and glared at them balefully until they left the room. They were headed back down the stairs when Reeves asked, "The library or the sunroom?"

To his disappointment, Anna grimaced. "I hate to say it, but I need to go. If I don't change my clothes soon I'll scream."

He could understand the sentiment. He felt the same way every evening when he came in from work. Still, it was a shame. She looked awfully good in that dress. And those shoes… Whoa.

"Lunch was interesting, to say the least. Will you thank your aunts for me?"

He put on a polite smile. "Sure. After I walk you to your car."

They slipped on their coats, and Reeves opened the door. Cold air and bright sunshine slapped them in equal measures. The light angled perfectly to slice beneath the overhang of the porch, which usually provided shade. They walked across the planking on the verandah to the top of the brick steps.

"So what did you think of the sermon?" he asked. He'd been wanting to know all afternoon.

She shrugged, pausing at the very edge of the porch. "I thought it was interesting. Except I didn't quite get what he meant about peace." She waved a hand. "The control of the mind…"

"The mind *controlled by* the Spirit," Reeves corrected gently.

"Is life and peace," she finished. "But what does that mean?" The way she said the word *peace* told him a lot. He gathered his words carefully.

"I know that when I can't find any peace it's because I'm not yielded to the control of the Holy Spirit. I just don't always know how to let go of whatever's cutting me up."

"How do you find out?"

Looking down, he admitted, "The hard way, usually."

She snorted at that. "Doesn't sound like you."

"Oh, yes, it does." Sighing, he looked her straight in the face. "Sometimes I think I do everything the hard way."

She shook her head, refusing to believe it, and that pleased him so much that he smiled and said, "Lately, though, it seems to have gotten a little easier. I seem to have acquired some wisdom from somewhere."

She considered then nodded. "I can see how your aunts might contribute to that."

He looked back at her in surprise. "True. But I was talking about you."

"Me?" She laughed as if it was a joke.

He spread his hands. "Anna, I've learned more about parenting my daughter from you than anyone else, ever."

Her jaw dropped. "Why, that can't be!"

"You've helped me understand how she thinks," he insisted, tapping his temple with his forefinger. "That's helped me change how I deal with her. What I wouldn't give to be able to read her as easily as you do."

"The only thing I do easily is make mistakes!" Anna exclaimed.

A bark of laughter escaped him. "Then that makes two of us. Though I suspect it's a universal problem."

"Why is it so easy to mess up and so hard to get things right?" she wondered.

"I don't know," Reeves told her, "but I suspect it has to do with what the pastor was talking about this morning. We don't keep our minds on the things of God as much as we should. Instead, we dwell on everything that can and has gone wrong, everything we can't do or mess up ourselves." Wow. Was he talking to her or himself?

Acknowledging his words with a pensive nod, she stepped down onto the brick. Aware that she was thinking over what he'd said, he took her by the elbow and led her down the remaining steps to the walkway.

"I think you're right," she said, "and I think that was exactly the message I needed to hear this morning."

"Funny," he said, "I was thinking the same thing about myself." They stepped onto the gravel, and he dropped his hand.

When she looked up, he expected another question. Instead, she said, "Thank you for the invitation to lunch."

"You're welcome." An idea popped into his head, and before he could even think it through, it was coming out of his mouth. "Say, why don't you come for a run with me in the morning?"

He hadn't known her eyes could go that wide. "Running? In the morning?"

"Yeah, I've started running in the morning rather than the evening so I can spend more time with Gilli." And not only was his daughter happy about it, his stress level at work had dropped precipitately.

"Oh. Um...well, what time?"

"Sixish?"

"S-s-s—" She coughed behind her fist. "Six." Nodding, she smiled. "In the morning?"

Delighted, he grinned and followed her around the car, telling her where to meet him in Buffalo Creek's expansive Chataugua Park.

"Maybe we can talk after," he suggested.

"About what?"

"Oh, I don't know. The database, if you've had a chance to look it over. I've got an idea I'd like to run by you, too."

"A-all right," she said, letting herself into her car. Smiling, she started up the battered little coupe and pulled away.

Pleased, Reeves waved farewell, but as he jogged back up the steps and into the house, the hard truth of Anna's earlier words came back to him.

The only thing I do easily is make mistakes.

Man, could he ever relate to that.

Maybe he was making a mistake right now, with her.

Or maybe it was time that he took this morning's sermon to heart, kept his mind on the things of God and allowed the Spirit to take control, for wherever God led was the right path. Suddenly he realized that his fears, doubts, assumptions and self-protective limits were just so much minutiae that he'd allowed to crowd out the things of God. No wonder he'd lost his way!

Lead me, O Lord, he thought, *and where You lead, I will follow. I want the kind of life that You want me to have. I won't try to make it happen myself this time, and I won't let the mistakes that I've made in the past hold me back from Your will. In Christ I am forgiven, and in Him I will do better, for myself, for Gilli. And for Anna.*

The database? Anna thought. He wanted to talk about that jam-packed folder of information he'd given her? After they went running at six o'clock in the blooming morning! Anna could not believe what she'd just agreed to. She couldn't get herself to work by eight, let alone haul her lazy behind out to a park by six a.m.!

"Say, why don't you come for a run with me in the morning?" she mimicked, sitting at a stop sign at the intersection of Chatam Boulevard and Main. She threw up her hands. "Sure! What time?" Banging her head on the steering wheel, she groaned. "Just kill me now."

The driver in the car behind her beeped his horn. She stomped the accelerator and winced as pain shot through her foot. That, she suspected, would soon be nothing by comparison. In the morning when she collapsed in an aching heap on the ground, Reeves would be all too aware that she was not who he evidently thought her to be.

She was nothing like him. Not only was she no spiritual giant, she couldn't run a business, couldn't run a relationship, couldn't run her own life, couldn't run, period. Maybe she could identify with Gilli, but that just made her the equivalent of a three-year-old! If she had a real brain in her head, she'd feign illness and beg off their running date before bedtime. Instead, she changed her clothes and went to buy running shoes. Then, in order to stay out of Tansy's way, she took the "dossier" to the coffee house and went through it line by line, cramming as if Reeves was going to give her an oral exam on the morrow.

Hours later, her brain clogged with data, Anna treated

herself to a hearty dinner. Afterward she went straight home to bed, where she replayed over and over everything that had been said, done and read throughout the entire day, from standing before her mirror that morning until she'd crawled between the sheets. Oddly, the thing that she kept circling back around to was that morning's sermon.

"The work of Christ on the cross set us free from the law of sin and death," the pastor had said. "That law demands sacrifice for sin, and should we die in our sin, without the cleansing of sacrifice, the law condemns us to true death, an eternity separated from God."

Jesus had made Himself the sacrifice, the pastor had explained. Perfect and without sin, He sacrificed His earthly body and life, once and for all, rising again to ascend into heaven and His rightful place.

"Do you want life?" the preacher had asked. "Accept the Lord's sacrifice."

That part Anna understood, but she'd never thought about what the preacher had said later.

"Fix your mind on Christ Jesus and keep it there. Learn everything He has to teach you through His word. Dwell in His Spirit so that when difficult times come you have the strength and the certainty to face them."

She remembered Reeves saying that he didn't always know how to let go of whatever was cutting him up. He'd termed it as not being yielded to the Holy Spirit. She wondered just what he meant by that. Did it have to do with fixing one's mind on Jesus?

She lay upon her bed and prayed as she had never prayed before, almost as if in conversation with her Lord. Her last thought as she finally slid into unconsciousness was that for the first time she didn't feel alone.

The alarm started going off at five. At half past, Anna finally hauled herself out of bed. After scrambling into her running gear, she hurried out to the car. Ten minutes later she stood within the inky shade of an immense hickory tree and watched Reeves stretch beneath the watery light of a vapor lamp perched high atop a pole beside a bench. The jogging track snaked through the trees and over the bridge that crossed the rambling creek that gave the town its name. He was already sweaty, his caramel-streaked nut brown hair darkened by perspiration, which meant that he'd been running for some time before she'd even gotten there.

"Oh, you are so out of your league," she told herself. "You're going to wind up in the emergency room." She wondered how many coronaries this track produced every year and deemed it a good thing that the hospital had been built nearby. Reeves straightened and waved. It was too late to rethink, so she picked up her feet, joining him just heart-beats later.

"Good morning," he called as she drew near.

"Morning."

A fellow with a big belly huffed by them. Obviously, she wasn't the only one out here freezing her toes off and courting a heart attack.

"Cold?" Reeves asked, and just the word spoken aloud made her shudder.

"Uh-huh."

"Let's get you warmed up then." He led her over to the bench. "Have you done this before?"

"Sure. About a decade ago in gym class. Whenever I couldn't get out of it."

Reeves chuckled. "Put your foot up on the seat and lean forward, keeping everything else straight."

She did as instructed. "Like this?"

"Looks right." He went down on his haunches and squeezed her calf. She nearly jumped over the bench. "Again," he ordered.

Her face flaming, she did as told until he decided that

she'd properly loosened up her muscles. Surprisingly, she already felt warmer.

"Now what?"

"Now we walk," he answered, nodding toward the narrow track.

Anna brightened immediately. Walking she could manage.

The track was just wide enough for them to walk side by side, their shoulders occasionally touching. He asked how her evening had gone. She shrugged and said that she'd spent it at the coffee shop then blathered on about how it was one of her favorite places and what her favorite drinks were and her favorite muffins, even her favorite barista, for pity's sake.

"She can make a perfect flower right in the center of the cup with the cream. Says she learned it in Seattle."

"Imagine that," Reeves replied with a grin. "Let's pick up the pace a bit."

Two minutes later, they were jogging and five minutes after that running. Reeves had the most fluid gait. It was impossible to stay even with their arms pumping in time to their strides, so she naturally fell back a bit, all the better to enjoy the show. The man's head stayed level while he ran, his long paces steady and gliding. She tried to match him stride for stride and found, to her surprise, that she could manage. For a time. And then she couldn't. Suddenly, without warning, she could no longer keep up. Just a minute or so later, she could no longer even breathe.

He seemed to know and slowed, but for Anna nothing would do but a full stop. Bending at the waist, she gasped for air. He jogged back to her and pulled her up straight, propelling her along the track again, this time at a walk.

"Come on. Walk it out. Otherwise you're going to hurt."

"As. Opposed. To. What?" she gasped out.

"As opposed to just being sore," he told her with a chuckle, slowing the pace.

After a while, she could breathe again. "I don't think I'm cut out for this," she told him, shaking her head.

"Ah, you're a natural," he refuted with a smile. "Take it from me. You just need a bit of conditioning. It would be nice to have a running buddy."

She groaned, but inside she was doing backflips. She was a natural at something? And they were going to be running buddies! Maybe. Why couldn't they have done this in high school? If he had shown just the least bit of interest in her back then she might have scrapped her rebellious habits just to please him. Then she might not have blown her chances at college by skipping senior finals week and settling for a D average.

Water under the bridge, she told herself. Sadly, it was too late for all that. Her life had been set in stone long ago.

He put her through the stretches again, and this time she watched as he did them and tried to copy his posture. Finally, she collapsed upon the bench. Reeves reached beneath a towel on the ground and brought up two bottles of water. He tossed her one, and she broke the seal, drinking greedily.

"Thanks."

"Yep."

They sat and slowly emptied the bottles, watching the sun come up and day gradually take over. Reeves hooked his elbows over the edge of the bench.

"I've had this idea I've been meaning to talk to you about."

"Oh? Something you didn't think to put in that portfolio?"

"Yeah." He waved a hand. "Just an idea. The only way I can think of to describe it is as a book without words."

"Come again?"

"You know, for toddlers, little kids like Gilli. I mean, they can't read, right? And I got to thinking about how you take a picture and make up a story about it."

"Well, that's just because of how I draw," she said dismissively. "Every time I lay down a sketch, I'm basically drawing a story in my head. Hmm." She bit her lip, thinking about that. "Actually, I have wondered what stories other people might dream up around one of my drawings."

"There. You see? It fits. What if you could come up with a series of drawings that suggest a story."

"But don't dictate it," she muttered to herself, envisioning a series of panels based on the skating ballerina concept.

"I'm sure there are parents who lack the imagination to utilize something like that," he admitted, "but—"

"Not many kids," she stated, feeling her excitement build.

"I knew I was onto something," Reeves declared. He stood then looked down at her. "Shall we talk this out over breakfast?"

She nodded eagerly, aware that a hole had opened in the bottom of her stomach during the past few minutes. She popped up with more energy than she'd expected to find. "Where do you want to go?"

He considered. "What time do you have to be at work?"

Work! She grabbed his arm and twisted it until she could read his watch. That could *not* be the time!

"Beans!" She lurched away, crying, "I'm going to be late!"

He put his hands to his waist, calling, "I guess that means breakfast is off?"

"Breakfast, lunch, maybe even dinner if I can't shower in five minutes flat!" she yelled.

She drove off and left him there, shaking his head. Dennis was not going to be a happy camper if she was late again. Depressing the accelerator, she took a deep breath.

"Fix your mind on Jesus," she whispered. "Fix your mind on Jesus."

Chapter Eleven

Reeves came in whistling that evening. The quartet of vehicles all but blocking the drive at the front of the house told him that the aunties were holding another of their meetings. They had clearly shifted into high gear with their plans for the fund-raiser. The place was like Grand Central Station. He'd run into one committee after another last week, and this week he expected it to be a daily occurrence, but today he didn't mind.

Gilli came through the side door just as he climbed out of the car and greeted him with a cheery, "Hi, Daddy!"

When he held out his arms, she literally leaped off the top step into them and gave him a noisy kiss. How wonderful it was to be loved by his baby girl! Hugging her close, he asked, "How's my sugar?"

"Goody good."

"Where's Special?"

"Getting her milk."

"I thought the vet said to go easy on the milk."

"But she already had 'nuff cans. Chester said she couldn't have no more."

"I see." As he carried Gilli into the house and set her on

her feet, he asked just how many cans of cat food she had served Special that day. She'd already proved that she could open the small pull-top tins with surprising ease.

Gilli shrugged evasively. "I dunno."

Reeves frowned. Wasn't a child who could learn to skate old enough to know better than to go into the pantry and help herself to all the cat food her schizophrenic pet wanted? "Do you remember how many the animal doctor said Special could have in a day?" Reeves asked, going down on his haunches to bring their faces level. Gilli just looked at him. He held up three fingers. "This many."

"Three," Gilli said, "like me."

Three. Old enough to be lonely without her daddy, not so old when indulging her first pet. "So how many did you give Special today?"

She held up four fingers, then five. When she got to six, she shrugged again and tucked her hands behind her. Reeves suppressed a sigh. A girl with a mommy-in-name-only could be forgiven for showering too much attention on a devoted animal. Still, there were boundaries. "From now on," he instructed, "you feed Special only what an adult gives you for her. Him."

Gilli nodded.

"The proper response is, 'Yes, sir,'" he coached.

"Yezer."

As she ran off to make sure Special had lapped up her—his!—fill of milk, Reeves made a mental note to tell Hilda to move all cat food to the top shelf of the pantry. Best make sure the milk was out of reach, too. Call it preventive parenting.

Making his way to the cloakroom, he hung up his coat before heading for the stairs. He wasn't the least surprised to find Tansy Burdett in the foyer. Naturally, he assumed that she served on one or more of his aunts' committees, but he also knew that she'd want to pump him for information about

Anna, information that he was determined not to give her. Nevertheless, he smiled congenially as he started up the steps.

"Hello, Mrs. Burdett. When you see my aunts will you tell them I've gone up to change please?"

Behind him, she said, "You took my granddaughter to church."

Reeves paused, telling himself not to respond, but then he turned to look down at her. "I did not. She took herself to church."

"You had something to do with it," Tansy insisted.

"I merely asked her why she didn't attend worship."

"And what did she say?"

He considered telling Tansy that she was the reason Anna had foregone worship, but he said instead, "What's important is that Anna decided to do the right, best thing."

The skepticism in Tansy's expression offended him on Anna's behalf. "But you brought her here to lunch afterward," Tansy insisted, as if she could not bear to give her granddaughter the benefit of the doubt. "And you were also seen jogging in the park together this morning."

"So? What of it?"

"So it seems to me that you are not as uninterested in my granddaughter as you first claimed."

Irritated, Reeves managed to speak calmly. "My interest in your granddaughter, or lack of it, is really none of your business." Turning, he stepped upward.

"I'll make it worth your while to marry her."

Reeves froze, wondering if he could possibly have heard Tansy correctly. Slowly he turned, his head tilting to one side. "Did you just try to bribe me to marry your granddaughter?"

Tansy looked him square in the eye. "Everyone thinks the Chatams are made of money, and they are. But you're a Leland, and there isn't enough money to go around in that branch."

Reeves glared at her until he was sure he had his temper under control. "I earn a comfortable living, thank you very much, and even if I didn't, no one marries for money in this day and age."

"Unless I miss my guess, the first Mrs. Leland did," Tansy said smugly.

That stung, but he couldn't argue with it. Besides, that was not important. Didn't she realize that something like this could only hurt Anna? He stepped back down to the foyer floor and demanded, "Why are you doing this?"

Tansy's face set in lines as hard as those of her too-yellow hair. "I want my granddaughter happily married. What's wrong with that?"

"It's her life. That's what's wrong with that."

Tansy's nose wrinkled in a sneer. "I've seen what she's done with her life. Trapped in a dead-end job, living in a dingy, depressing apartment too small to turn around in, no real friends, a date once in a blue moon. The one saving grace is that she hasn't tried to drown herself in alcohol or snort her problems up her nose the way her parents did."

"I don't call that a small thing," Reeves stated flatly, "and neither is your interference in Anna's life."

Tansy lifted her chin, shoulders squared like a general. "Someone has to do something, and I know what's best for my granddaughter. She needs a husband. You seem to have a beneficial influence on her, and she always did have a crush on you."

"That's ridiculous."

"You really don't know?" Tansy chuckled. "I thought you were smarter than that. When she was a teenager I used to find sheets of torn notebook paper in her trash can." She mimicked handwriting. "Mrs. Reeves Leland. Anna Leland. Reeves and Anna Leland."

Reeves must have gaped at her for a full minute. Anna had had a crush on him in high school? That's what all that torment was about? Surely not. But what if that had been the case? How mortified would Anna be after keeping that secret all these years? He went straight from shock to outrage in three seconds flat. "How dare you reveal such a thing? Have you no respect for your granddaughter?"

"I thought you knew. Besides, what does it hurt? The truth is the truth."

"If it's true, then it's Anna's truth," he insisted. "She's entitled to decide if and when she reveals her secrets. In fact she's entitled to make her own decisions about everything, period. To make such a revelation to further your own cause is cold and heartless."

Tansy jerked as if he'd struck her, bawling, "I'm not heartless. I only want what's best for my granddaughter!"

"You want what *you* want," he rebutted, his voice rising, "to the point of trying bribery! That's not just selfish, it's sick!" The sudden appearance of the aunties in the foyer was enough to forestall further explosion, but Reeves wasn't about to back down.

Tansy stood with military stoicism, shoulders back, chin up. "I know my granddaughter," she declared defensively.

"You know nothing about Anna," he told her. "You say I've been a 'beneficial influence' on her, but it's actually the other way around. Anna's the one who's had a 'beneficial influence,' on me."

"I certainly see no evidence of it," Tansy snapped. The aunties gasped. Tansy's chin ratcheted up another inch or so.

"Then I'm sure you want better for Anna than me," Reeves said evenly. "Anna certainly deserves better."

"I'm more concerned with what she needs, and I'll do what I have to do to see that she gets it," Tansy vowed. With that, she executed a neat about-face and marched into the parlor. Casting worried, apologetic glances behind them, Magnolia and Odelia hurried after her.

"I'm so sorry, dear," Hypatia said to Reeves, rushing

forward. "We had no idea what she was up to when she left the room, but it's all our fault, just the same. If we hadn't planted that ridiculous notion about you and Anna in her head…"

Anna Leland. Anna and Reeves Leland.

In some ways it felt as if his world had turned upside down. And in some ways it felt as if it had been turned right side up!

Hypatia wrung her hands. "Oh, poor Anna. I'm afraid we've set Tansy off on a new tangent. We have to fix this. Is it possible, do you think, to convince Tansy that this scheme of hers is hopeless?"

Reeves shook his head, still reeling. "I don't know."

"We have to try. We started this. We have to stop it. Don't you think so?"

"I—I'm not sure," Reeves admitted, barely attending. Had Tansy always been this controlling? Yes, of course, she had. In fact, she'd probably been worse. No wonder Anna had left home at the first opportunity.

"What if we got everyone together and hashed this out?" Hypatia was saying. "All of us together, we might make Tansy see reason, don't you think? It might nip Tansy's meddling in the bud. At the very least, Anna would know that she has support. It would need much prayer to work, of course. Much prayer."

Prayer. Reeves nodded absently, wearied by the weight of his anger at Tansy and a growing sense of all-too-familiar guilt.

Mrs. Reeves Leland. Anna Leland. Anna and Reeves Leland.

She had liked him. Liked him. And he'd assumed the very opposite.

Hadn't it been the same with Gilli? Every time she'd misbehaved, he'd assumed on some level that she hated him for letting her mommy leave, and all along she'd been doing everything in her power to grab his attention and hold it. He hadn't seen it until the bees had driven Nanny away and brought them here to Chatam House where they'd met Anna. Anna, who had taught him so much about his daughter—and himself. Anna whom he had treated so disdainfully in the past.

"Should I do it then?" Hypatia's voice interrupted his thoughts. He looked down at her blankly.

"Uh, whatever you think best."

She bit her lip and nodded as if still uncertain. Not really cognizant of Hypatia's concerns, Reeves let it go. Who could be more competent than Aunt Hypatia, after all? As he mounted the stairs once more, his thoughts sought heavenly counsel.

Father in heaven, I've been such a lunkhead. All those years that I judged Anna's behavior so harshly, when I had no idea what she was dealing with, no understanding of her at all, when a kind word from me might have made a difference, a ride in my car in the rain, a friendly gesture, a smile of acknowledgment... But I did none of those things. And after all of that, she still found it within her heart to take my little girl under her wing, to reach out to me in friendship and honesty. What a fool I have been.

God forgive him.

And Anna, too. If she could.

"And how are you this afternoon?" The voice of Reeves Leland traveled over the telephone line, through the receiver, into her ear and across her every nerve ending with a rush of heat.

Anna turned her back to the workroom and kept her voice low. With Dennis on the rampage again, it wouldn't do to get caught mooning over a caller.

"In hot water," she muttered.

"You're not talking about soaking away your muscle aches, I assume."

Every muscle in Anna's body had screamed when she'd crawled into the tub last night, but this morning she'd only felt a few twinges as she'd showered, dressed and headed out. She should have made it to work with minutes to spare, but no. She had to get stuck at one of the town's many railroad crossings by the longest train in history. Did that matter to Dennis, though? Not one bit.

"I feel fine. It's a work thing."

"I hope it's not this call. Some workplaces have a rule about personal calls, I know, but I tried to call you at home last night only your number's unlisted."

Personal calls. She had to quip around her heart, which had leaped up into her throat. "Yeah, I know. It infuriates Tansy that she has to stop by to harangue me."

He did not laugh, not even a chuckle. "I'll keep it brief," he said after a pause. "Are you up for a run tomorrow morning?"

Anna put her hand over her mouth to hide her pleased smile, but then she deflated. If she was late for work one more time, Dennis would can her for sure, especially with the BCBC job winding down. Should she risk it?

Reeves went on in a coaxing voice. "I was out there all by myself today. Not nearly so much fun without a buddy."

Anna grit her teeth to keep from saying yes. Maybe if they started a little earlier… Right. Like she could manage that. It took a good half hour to get her brain started in the morning.

"Oh, man. I just don't think I can do it."

For several seconds Reeves said nothing then, "Anna, if I've done anything, recently or in the past—"

"What? No, no, no." She hated to tell him that she couldn't trust herself to get to work on time. If she were more conscientious or more mature or just more of a morning person, she'd be able to manage an early run, but right now, having been late twice in a row, it was just asking for trouble. "This is on me. I'm just not, you know, cut out for early morning activity." She thought of Gilli and added, "But you, now, you need your evenings free for your daughter."

Maybe, she thought, when Dennis got off the warpath she could try again. She'd just tell Reeves that she'd changed her mind and decided that she needed to get into shape. Right then she made a plan. Starting tonight she was going to go to bed and get up an hour earlier every day, and just to be on the safe side, she'd set the clocks in the apartment forward by fifteen minutes, too. She'd train herself to get up earlier and be out on that jogging trail in a couple weeks.

"Maybe I can call you sometime anyway," Reeves said after a bit. "Just to hear an adult voice, you know? I mean, it won't be long now before we'll be back in our own place, just the two of us, Gilli and me."

"Sure," Anna answered brightly. "Anytime you need to hear an adult voice." She waited two seconds. "I can always turn on the television and lay the phone next to it."

He laughed, finally. "I'll remember that."

"Great, and do a favor for me, will you? Tell your aunts that I'll be around with the final print run tomorrow."

"They'll be happy to hear it."

"Tell them to expect me around noon," she said, thinking that it wouldn't hurt her cause with Dennis any if she made the delivery on her lunch hour rather than during the workday.

"I'll tell them," he said softly.

"Thanks." She rang off with a cheery, "Later, alligator," but then she hugged herself, wondering just how long she'd have to wait for that next call.

Reeves hung up the phone and leaned back in his desk chair, regret weighing heavily in his chest. Well, that answered that. Whether she'd had a crush on him all those years ago or not, Anna obviously didn't think of him that way any longer. If she did, she'd have accepted his invitation. Not a morning person, she'd basically said. Yet, she'd been out there once already, and she'd put forth a fine performance, too. Apparently, the company had not been worth the effort, however.

Well, what was a high school crush, anyway? They never lasted, rarely turned into anything real. Had he not been stupid as a fence post all those years ago—and all those between then and now, for that matter—he might have treated her a little more kindly. They might have come away friends, at least. Instead, in his judgmental mind they'd been enemies. He finally saw her for who and what she was, someone admirable, strong and true, clever, beautiful, giving… She saw him as…what? Unworthy of her time and effort. Never let it be said that his was not a just God.

"Okay, Lord," he prayed aloud, "if that's how You want it. You know best."

Didn't mean he liked it, of course, but he couldn't help thinking that if he'd had that attitude about Marissa, he most likely wouldn't have married her. Of course, then he wouldn't have Gilli. It occurred to him that he hadn't heard from Marissa lately. Maybe she'd finally figured out that he wasn't going to offer her money to stay away, not that he wouldn't prefer that. As long as she was Gilli's mother, though, Gilli needed to see her.

Right now he was more likely to pay Marissa to make Gilli think she cared. Of course, if he did give Marissa money, she could use it to make his life miserable by hiring a lawyer and petitioning the court for physical custody. She wouldn't win, but it would it be a huge headache, which she undoubtedly knew, one he might be willing to pay to avoid. No doubt that was her game. On the other hand…

He shook his head. What did it say, he wondered, that he'd rather fill his head with useless speculation about Marissa than admit how much it hurt for Anna to refuse to go running with him? Nothing good. He very much feared that it said nothing good. Regret, it seemed, was to be his companion, one way or another, for the rest of his days.

Sunshine as clear as glass picked out bits of green in the straw-brown lawn in front of Chatam House. The heady scent of spring kissed the slight breeze that chilled the warming air. It was about time, Anna remarked to herself, scooping the stacked boxes on the backseat of her car into her arms. In true Texas fashion, the change in the weather had actually been startling. Only two days had passed since she'd met Reeves in the park for their run, but those two days had seemed like weeks.

She carried the boxes of auction catalogs to the front door, where she managed to hit the doorbell button with an elbow. It opened almost instantly. Magnolia said not a word in greeting, just turned back into the house and called, "Anna's here!"

Anna stepped into the foyer behind her and kicked the door closed with her foot. Odelia appeared, garbed in a flowered shirtwaist and pearl white cardigan, with what looked like yellow tennis balls sprouting from her earlobes. She clasped her hands together beneath her chubby, cleft chin and cried out, "Anna Miranda, how lovely!"

Hypatia arrived on the scene next, rushing and murmuring, "Excellent. Excellent." The three of them quickly divested Anna of the boxes, which they deposited on the foyer table. "You're just in time for lunch."

"Oh, no," Anna said. She should have realized when she'd chosen to deliver the material during her lunch hour that the Chatams would have a meal waiting on her. Suddenly, Gilli flew down the hall and barreled into her, arms outstretched.

"Anna, Anna!"

She staggered back, catching the girl in a crouching hug. "Hey, munchkin."

"Do you like fishy salad?" Gilli asked excitedly.

"Tuna salad," Magnolia corrected.

Actually, Anna loathed tuna salad. Tuna itself she had no problem with, but any fish mixed up with mayonnaise and whatever else, no, thanks.

"I'm afraid I grabbed a hot dog on the way over here," she said evasively. A chili cheese dog, in fact, eaten behind the wheel of her car.

The Chatams murmured regrets, but those got lost in Gilli's announcement.

"Special loves fishy salad!"

Hypatia gasped, and Magnolia moaned as Odelia hurried down the hall and through the dining room door, screeching, "No, cat! No! Get off that table!"

Magnolia looked at Hypatia, her cheeks rather pale. "Hot dogs sound good. I wonder if Hilda has any." She quickly trundled off toward the kitchen.

Anna cleared her throat to keep from laughing, as Hypatia was clearly not amused. Hypatia looked down at Gilli and instructed smartly, "I want you to take that cat upstairs and lock it in your suite, Gilli Leland, and I don't care if it howls its head off."

Gilli's lip puffed out, and for an instant Anna feared she was going to argue, but even a child could tell when Hypatia Chatam had reached her limit. "'Kay, Auntie 'Patia," Gilli murmured, running off to the dining room.

Hypatia sighed. "The adventures of housing a cat," she said with a strained smile.

"Sorry about lunch," Anna ventured.

"It's not lunch I'm really concerned about," Hypatia said staunchly. "We were wondering if you'd come to dinner on Friday evening?"

Anna smiled. "Of course. I'd love to. Thank you for asking."

The cat yowled, and Hypatia put a hand to her head. "We've, ah, become so fond of you," she said, "and you've done such wonderful work for us."

"It was my pleasure," Anna told her honestly, "and I was paid. You don't have to go out of your way to thank me, you know."

"Well, it's not that exactly," Hypatia began, over the sounds of scrambling from the dining room. "Although we are very grateful, you understand. It's more of a…" Odelia yelped, and Hypatia floundered. "That is, well, Reeves and…" She cast a worried glance at the dining room door.

"Reeves will be here at dinner on Friday?" Anna pressed hopefully.

Hypatia glanced at her, "Yes, yes. Didn't I just say so?"

Clearing her throat, Anna did her best not to beam. "What time should I arrive?"

Suddenly the most awful caterwauling came from the dining room. Hypatia winced and replied succinctly, "Six-thirty."

Assuming that a cat fight, in the truest sense of the term, was about to break out, Anna reached for the scrolled doorknob. "I'll see you then."

"Wonderful," Hypatia said, turning away. "Do excuse me."

Anna danced out onto the veranda, pulling the door closed behind her. Looked like she wouldn't have to sit home indefinitely waiting for that phone call, after all. She could, in fact, just tell Reeves on Friday that she'd changed her mind about those early morning runs. What was a job compared to spending time with Reeves Leland, anyway? If she stuck to her plan, he might well get busy and never call her. It wouldn't be the first time that had happened. And who knew where those morning runs might one day lead? This, after all, was not high school any longer.

She never dreamed that she might soon wish otherwise.

Chapter Twelve

Tansy showed up on Anna's doorstep at eight o'clock the next evening.

"I just want to be sure that you understand the significance of tomorrow's dinner," she announced, practically pushing her way inside the apartment.

Puzzled, Anna closed the door and turned to stand in front of it, her arms folded. "What would you know about it?"

"I know that you need a husband, and Reeves Leland is the ideal candidate," Tansy said, lifting her chin and smiling slyly.

Anna's jaw dropped. "I don't *need* a husband!" And if she did, Reeves would not be applying for the position.

"As if your job isn't hanging by a thread this very instant," Tansy scoffed.

"I can always get another job." In fact, she'd been thumbing through that dossier Reeves had given her. There were work-from-home positions that would allow her to concentrate on a new project she'd started, a project also inspired by Reeves.

"You wouldn't need a job if you had a husband," Tansy proclaimed.

Anna gaped, boggled by this new interest in her marital status. "That's nonsense. Husbands are more than paychecks, and lots of wives work. Besides, do you think I'd marry just so I could quit my job?"

"I think you'd marry for any reason at all if the right man asked you."

"The *right* man," Anna stressed, "not *any* man who could support me."

Tansy threw up her hands. "That's what I said! Why are you always arguing about nothing? You live to argue about nothing!"

"And you live to dictate to me!" Anna shot back. She slashed her arms down angrily. "I'm not going to debate this. You don't know what you're talking about anyway. Reeves isn't interested in me like that." It pained her to say it, but it was the truth. Even if he had kissed her that one time.

Gratitude, she reminded herself. Simple gratitude.

Still, he had invited her to go running. That wasn't exactly a date, but it could change, given time—and provided Tansy didn't get involved.

"He could be," Tansy was saying, "if you played your cards right." She swept a scathing glance over Anna's comfy sweats. "Wear something feminine. Like that dress you wore to church."

Anna rolled her eyes. That day had been a special case. She'd feel like a complete fool waltzing in there Friday evening in heels and nylons. That was not her usual style, and everyone at Chatam House well knew it by now.

"And don't worry," Tansy went on. "The rest of us will be there to smooth over any gaffes."

"The rest of us?" Anna yelped. "You won't be there."

"Oh, but I will." Tansy gave her a long look. "We're in agreement on this."

"We?" Anna stared at Tansy's smug smile, feeling the blood drain out of her head.

"Me and the Chatam sisters. They agree that Reeves could be the best thing to ever happen to you."

Anna actually felt light-headed. "You got the Chatams to set this up?"

"Dinner was actually Hypatia's idea," Tansy said, looking away, "but I believe that it's a wise course of action, especially if you take my advice to heart. For pity's sake, just try to fix the man's interest, will you? I've done my best to pave the way, give you a real opportunity with him."

"Opportunity," Anna echoed, horrified.

"It's what you've always wanted, isn't it? Since high school you've been dreamy-eyed over him."

Anna gasped. *Please, God, no.* That had been her secret, her one real secret. She couldn't bear it if her grandmother knew about her idiotic crush. And yet, she seemed to.

"Opportunity?" Anna repeated in angry disbelief. "You think you've engineered an opportunity to get me and Reeves together? What you've really done is ruined it! Even if he might have one day looked at me as someone he could love, I would never give you the satisfaction of falling in with your plans!"

Tansy reared back. "You can't be so idiotic as to not take what you want just to thwart me!"

"Can't I?" Anna cried, teetering on the edge of self-control. "Thwarting you has been my lifelong ambition! Isn't that what you've always said?" She reached behind her and yanked open the door. "Get out of my apartment!"

Something flashed across Tansy's face, not disappointment precisely or even sadness but something close to both. "I thought you'd be pleased," she said in a strange voice. "For once I actually thought you'd be pleased."

Anna refused to even think about what that look and that voice meant. All she wanted was for Tansy to leave before she dissolved into blubbering tears. To her relief, Tansy did just that, trudging through the door with her head down.

Anna slammed it closed behind her and threw the deadbolt for good measure, then she collapsed into the chair in the corner.

Tansy and the Chatam sisters had plotted to bring her and Reeves together? Anna had always known, of course, that the Chatams were friends with her grandmother, but she'd never dreamed that they would stoop to Tansy's level of manipulation. She thought of all those late afternoon appointments when Reeves just happened to arrive home from work. Tansy must have put the idea in their heads. Oh, good grief. Had Tansy told them about that ridiculous crush? She clapped her hands over her ears as if that alone could undo their hearing of it.

"Dear God," she whispered, "Oh, dear God, please." But she already knew.

It really was ruined. She could never show her face at Chatam House or to Reeves Leland again.

The last thing Reeves wanted to do after a long Friday at work was stop by the grocery store to pick up tea bags, but he had his reasons. For one, it was the least he could do for his poor, put-upon aunts. The cat raid on the tuna salad the previous day had resulted in banishment—for both Special and Gilli, who had adamantly refused to leave their suite without her beloved pet. Everyone had been so upset that he'd thought it best to take dinner with her and Special in their rooms last evening. Today, fortunately, had offered no repeat of the previous day's events. He'd called home half a dozen times to make sure of it.

Cars jammed the parking lot of the aunties' preferred grocery. It was rush hour at the supermarket, with everyone just off work and trying to stock up for the weekend. Reeves consoled himself with the expectation of seeing Anna again over dinner in less than two hours. He'd been disappointed to be rebuffed when he'd called to ask her to go running again, so he'd been glad to learn on his way out the door this morning that the aunties had invited her to dinner tonight.

He wasn't sure what had occasioned the invitation, but he was grateful that they'd issued it. He wanted a chance to change Anna's mind about him. An apology might even be in order, if he could manage to explain his regretful behavior without revealing Tansy's deplorable tactics. Anna would no doubt be hurt by her grandmother's thoughtless, heavy-handed actions. Hopefully tonight's dinner would give him a perfect opportunity to make amends. Therefore, stop for tea bags, he would.

If he could somehow also find time to get by his house before dinner, he'd have his whole evening free, and his meeting tomorrow morning with the remodeling contractor would go much more quickly. Then maybe he and Gilli could actually do something fun this weekend to stay out of the aunties' hair. He wondered if they might find a movie that they could both enjoy. And if Anna might want to enjoy it with them. After his dealings with Tansy, his admiration for Anna had grown. He felt strongly that she deserved whatever enjoyment he and Gilli could give her.

Reeves found a parking spot far back in the lot and hiked in. He fought his way through a crowd gathered around the carts and another at the deli counter then cut through a side aisle to the correct section of the store. Finding the right brand required some minutes. The aunties were particular about their tea, but after living in their house these past weeks, even he was beginning to note the subtle differences in blends.

Finally, with the nearly weightless packet firmly in hand, he started toward the checkout, only to find one aisle after another clogged with shoppers pushing carts. He decided to cut all the way across to the frozen food section and skirt around the busy center of the store. Passing by the ice cream, he quickly turned down the frozen food aisle—and bumped smack into Anna.

They collided hard enough to knock the frozen entrée that she was examining out of her hand, and both instantly went down to retrieve it. Reeves snagged it first, owing to his longer arms.

"Glad to have run into you," he quipped.

"Sorry," she muttered, reaching for the small cardboard carton.

"Here you go." He returned it to her with a chuckle and drew her up to her feet, his hand beneath her elbow. "Not that you need it," he told her with a grin. "I hear Hilda's cooking a pork loin for our dinner."

"*Your* dinner," Anna retorted. Turning toward the freezer, she yanked open the glass door and practically tossed the frozen entrée inside before reaching for another.

Reeves felt a *thunk* inside his chest, and several things occurred to him at once. First, she was angry, and not because he had bumped into her. Second, she was shopping for her dinner. Third, she wouldn't even look at him. Obviously, had she ever intended to come to Chatam House that evening, it would not have been to see him. That last stood out with painful clarity, but it all culminated in one conclusion.

"You're not coming."

Mutely, she shook her head.

"Why not? I'm sure my aunts are expecting you."

She snorted. "Me and my grandmother. Did you think I would go once I found out how Tansy had manipulated everything?"

Reeves winced. "You know about that?"

Anna hung her head, muttering, "She told me last night."

He clenched his fist and brought it to the center of his forehead. What was wrong with Tansy Burdett? Did she actively seek to hurt Anna? So much for only wanting what was best for her granddaughter!

"Anna, I'm so sorry," he said, dropping his hand. "I hoped you wouldn't find out."

She gaped at him. "You were going along with it?"

"No! How could you think I'd take her money?"

"Her money? Don't you mean her granddaughter? That's what she wants, you know, to get us together."

"How could I not when she offered me money to marry you?"

Anna goggled, her eyes going impossibly wide. "You're telling me she offered you *money* to *marry me?*"

Reeves clamped a hand over his mouth. She hadn't known!

"I—I thought…when you said you knew about her manipulation…"

"Of dinner tonight! We were all supposed to eat together."

He shook his head, trying to make sense of this. "All? Wait. Tansy, too?"

"Of course, Tansy, too! They're all in it together, my grandmother and your aunts. I'm somehow supposed to, quote, fix your interest, unquote."

Reeves moaned. He couldn't say that the aunties would never do such a thing because, after all, they had already dabbled in matchmaking between him and Anna, but he was shocked that they would involve Tansy, especially after that scene at Chatam House on Monday evening.

"I can't believe…" His voice trailed off as he recalled Hypatia saying something about trying to convince Tansy that her plan was hopeless. "Wait a minute. That's not what this is about."

Anna's face set. "But my grandmother specifically said—"

"That's Tansy's agenda for tonight," Reeves interrupted firmly. "My aunts have something else entirely in mind, I'm sure of it." He tapped his temple with the tip of one forefinger, trying to recall Hypatia's exact words, something about convincing Tansy and supporting Anna. "It was after I blasted Tansy for mentioning the crush."

Anna gasped. "She…she told you?"

"What?"

"She told you!" Anna warbled, tears filling her eyes. Before he could ask her to explain, she dropped the frozen entrée and ran.

"Anna!"

Ignoring him, she disappeared around the corner. Stunned, Reeves looked at the flimsy packet of tea bags in his hand. Then he simply tossed it and went after her.

Anna ran blindly through the supermarket, stumbling into people and careening around carts and displays in a desperate bid to get away from the mortifying truth. Her grandmother had tried to bribe a man to marry her, and of course it had to be the only man she'd ever cared about! Even worse, Reeves knew how she'd pined for him, how she'd hoped and prayed and dreamed that he would look her way and finally truly see her. The humiliation was worse than anything Anna had ever imagined.

She got to her car and reached for the door handle before realizing that the keys were still in the pocket of her jeans. She was trying to dig them out when a hand clamped down on her shoulder and spun her around.

"I'm sorry."

She shook her head. What did he have to be sorry about? It was all Tansy's fault. It was always Tansy's fault. Capturing her with his hands, he splayed his fingers in her hair, his palms covering her ears.

"I'm sorry I hurt you. I didn't know. I didn't understand what it must have been like for you."

Anna felt her face burning. She couldn't think, couldn't reason. All she could do was shake her head. He dropped his hands to her shoulders, gripping hard to hold her in place because she couldn't seem to stand still.

"I'm sorry, Anna, for all those years that I judged your

behavior without ever understanding the reason for it. I finally realized what you were fighting, how hard you worked to stand up to her."

Anna brought her hands to her head, struggling to think and coming up against the same awful idea. He knew. He knew her most carefully guarded secret. "What e-exactly d-did she tell you?"

"After she attempted to bribe me, you mean?"

Anna rolled her eyes at that. "Of all the stupid…I mean, like that was going to work. You're a Chatam, for goodness' sake."

"I'm a Leland," he corrected dryly, his grip on her shoulders intensifying, "and the Lelands don't actually have any money."

"What difference does it make?" Anna asked, shrugging his hands away with thoughtless impatience. "It's not like you care about that."

"No," he said rather cheerfully, "I don't." Grinning, he leaned forward and said, "And neither do you."

She looked up at him, tired of this runaround. She had to know. "What did Tansy say to you?"

Reeves smiled sympathetically. "About the, um, crush, you mean?"

Wincing, Anna squeezed her eyes closed. Maybe she didn't want to know, after all. Maybe she ought to just crawl under the car and stay there until he either went away or she died of starvation, whichever came first. Too late.

"She said she found notebook paper," he told her softly, "that you'd written some names on. Anna Leland. Anna and Reeves Leland."

"Oh-oh-oh." Anna reeled, coming up hard against the side of her car.

Talk about stupid! How many sheets of paper had she filled with that drivel? *Mrs. Anna Leland. Mrs. Reeves Leland. Anna Miranda Leland. Reeves and Anna Leland…*

And she'd thought she'd been so clever, tearing the pages into tiny pieces, hiding them in closets and under floorboards, while Tansy undoubtedly had known all along.

And now Reeves knew. Probably his aunts, too.

Moaning, Anna covered her face with her hands and did her best to disappear. After a long moment, she heard shoe soles scrape against the pavement, and then something brushed against her hair.

"Anna?" he queried softly.

"Go away," she choked out.

"No."

She balled her hands into fists. "Please just go away."

"Not until you listen to me."

Here it comes, she thought, the useless dismissals. She could already hear them. *It wouldn't have worked out. We're too different. I was heading off to college. It wasn't real love, just a silly schoolgirl crush.* All the things she'd told herself a countless number of times, he would now tell her. Maybe they would finally work. Maybe, after all these years, she could finally just get over it.

She dropped her hands and opened her eyes, ready for the volley, ready to take the truth right in the heart.

"I can't have you thinking ill of my aunts," he said. "They only wanted to try to derail your grandmother. I think they feel responsible for having discussed among themselves that you would be a wonderful mother for Gilli."

Anna blinked, a rush of warm surprise flowing through her. "They said that?"

One corner of his lips quirked. "A number of times. That seems to have given Tansy the idea to get us together, and we may have added fuel to the fire ourselves."

"Last Sunday at church."

"Mmm. Hypatia hoped that they and I and you together could make Tansy see that…" He seemed momentarily at a loss for words, but he shifted his stance slightly and went on.

"That she's driven you away with her obsessive need to control your life."

"Fat chance!" Anna huffed, folding her arms.

"Yeah," Reeves said, "she's nothing if not determined, this grandmother of yours, and she obviously has her own agenda for this dinner. *Her* agenda," he reiterated, "not ours. I propose that we just don't play her game."

"As if I ever have."

He grinned and tapped her on the end of the nose. "Exactly."

Narrowing her eyes at him, she cut him an incisive glance. "What are you suggesting?"

"For starters, that neither of us show up for dinner. The aunties will understand, and it'll throw a spoke in Tansy's wheel. Then…" He shrugged. "We'll figure it out."

Anna wondered what was left to figure out, but she didn't ask. She was still trying to reason through Reeves's behavior. He hadn't said a word about her ridiculous crush. Maybe he figured it was too silly to bother about, water under the bridge, over and done with years and years ago.

Suddenly he asked, "Do you know where my house is?"

Taken off guard, she simply nodded.

"Good. I'll meet you there in an hour, less if I can manage it. Okay?"

She opened her mouth, but so many questions crowded her tongue that she couldn't sort through them to get at the right one.

He shook her gently. "Okay?"

She blinked and gave him the answer he seemed to want. "Okay."

Beaming a smile at her, he hurried back toward the store. "Less than an hour, I promise. Then we'll talk."

Anna hugged herself, watching him dart through traffic back toward the building, his tie flapping in beat to his movements. Even after he disappeared through the automatic sliding doors, she stood there, slightly dazed by the emotional upheaval of the past few minutes. Finally, she pulled her keys from her pocket and let herself into the car. Slumping down behind the steering wheel, she tried to gather her thoughts.

What, she wondered, did he expect to talk about? Her embarrassment at Tansy's highhandedness? *His* embarrassment at Tansy's high-handedness? *Not high school and all that, please God.*

On the other hand, what if he wanted to just talk, period, about…whatever normal people talk about? Was that possible?

He'd apologized for judging her. If she apologized for having made his life a misery all those years ago, that would be a start toward…friendship, at least. Wouldn't it?

There was only one way to find out.

Reeves let himself into Chatam House via the side door, as usual, carrying the retrieved packet of tea in one hand. The sound of running footsteps greeted him perhaps two seconds before his daughter launched herself at him out of the gloom of the hallway.

"Daddy!"

He caught her up and parked her on his hip, hugging her close. "Hi, sugar." She smelled fresh and sweet and wore clean clothes, a matching set of royal blue knit top and pants. "You look pretty."

"Anna's coming."

"Ooh, I don't think so," he told her, carrying her through the house, "but you and I are going to see her, instead."

She tilted her head, caramel curls bouncing. "Can Special come?"

"Uh, no. Special will have to stay here."

Sighing, Gilli spread her hands in a gesture of helplessness. "I ha'fa stay wif her."

"Gilli, you can't stay with that cat all the time."

"I promise her, Daddy, 'cause Aunt 'Patia say she gots to stay in the kitchen for our dinner party."

"Yes, I know about the aunts' dinner party," Reeves said absently, turning down the central hall.

"No, I mean in the kitchen, me and Chester and Hilda and Carol and Special."

Ah, so that was Hyaptia's plan, a very clever one that would effectively keep Gilli and the cat out of the way. "I see. Well, if that's what you want to do, then I'll give Anna your regrets."

Gilli screwed up her face. "What's grets?"

"*Re*grets. It means that I'm sorry I won't be able to join you."

"Oh. That's 'kay." She patted him as if accepting his apology.

Reeves grinned and carried her into the parlor, where he paused to set her on her feet before addressing the others gathered there.

"Hello, everyone." He moved from spot to spot, kissing cheeks until all three of his aunts had been greeted, then stood before Tansy and acknowledged her with a nod that was almost a bow. Ignoring Tansy's wide smile, he turned back to Hypatia and dropped the box of tea into her lap. "As requested."

"Thank you, dear."

"You're welcome. Unfortunately, I won't be around to enjoy your special tea this evening. In fact, I'm afraid I won't be able to stay for dinner, either."

Behind him, Tansy barked, "What?"

Hypatia looked troubled. "That is a shame."

He grinned. "Sorry, I have other plans." He bent to hug her in sheer gratitude for the lovely, godly woman that she was. "Don't count on Anna, either," he whispered.

"Oh?"

He straightened with a wink. "Mmm-hmm. I hope that's all right with you."

Hypatia smiled. "Of course. God's plans always supercede our own."

He grinned at her. "Couldn't agree more." Maybe this was all part of God's plan. Maybe God had been the real matchmaker all along. If so, He wouldn't let Tansy scuttle things. "I hope it's okay if Gilli stays here. I understand there's a dinner party in the kitchen that she doesn't want to miss."

Hypatia lifted her eyebrows. "I insist that Gilli stay. She's our only hope for a peaceful meal."

Laughing, Reeves turned with an expansive sweep of his arm to take his leave of the others. "Enjoy, my lovelies!" With that he bounded from the room, feeling ridiculously pleased. He couldn't have arranged things better himself.

As he moved toward the stairs, he heard Tansy hiss, "Make him stay!"

"He's an adult," Hypatia returned firmly. "We can't and wouldn't try to *make* him do anything."

Grinning, Reeves climbed the stairs two at a time. He didn't know why he felt so ebullient, and just now he didn't care. Thinking of Anna, he quickly changed into jeans, a black long-sleeved T-shirt and casual shoes before grabbing a denim jacket and heading back downstairs, where he kissed his little girl—and at her insistence, her cat—goodbye. He figured he came away with his face intact merely because Gilli was holding the vicious thing at the time.

Ten minutes later, he pulled up in front of his house to find Anna waiting for him, dressed exactly as before in jeans and a double T-shirt but with the addition of a snug little cardigan. Leaning against the fender of her pathetic coupe with her arms folded, she frowned solemnly; yet he smiled, absolutely delighted to see her.

This woman, he realized, was not just his friend, she was his best friend, someone to be admired, someone who deserved regard and kindness. She had enriched his life and that of his daughter in ways that he could not have imagined. He shook his head, hardly able to believe it.

The brat had become one of his greatest blessings, and very possibly, he realized with a jolt, the answer to his prayers.

Chapter Thirteen

They dined on pizza at Gilli's favorite restaurant, though Gilli had elected to stay at home with her cat. Anna smiled at Reeves's animated account of Gilli's dedication to her pet and Tansy's outraged disappointment as his defection. She listened carefully to his frank description of his encounters—two, as it turned out—with Tansy, and felt a certain sense of vindication at what he said afterward.

"I knew she was difficult, but I figured it was just a quirk of her personality, a first impulse sort of thing. I never realized how far she would go to try to dictate to you or why you would rebel so blatantly. I just want you to know, I get it now."

Anna nodded then shrugged, still troubled by a sense of Tansy controlling her. "She always manages to set it up so she gets her way. Like right now."

"How do you mean?"

Spreading her hands, Anna stated the obvious. "She wanted to get us together, and here we are."

"On our terms," Reeves pointed out, "not hers."

"Still, Tansy gets what Tansy wants."

He reached across the table and captured one of her hands.

"Anna, you've got to stop this," he said. "It's about what *you* want and what's best for you, not what Tansy wants or thinks is best. If the two should happen to be one and the same, you can't let the fact that it pleases Tansy mess up everything. I thought you got that when you showed up at church. Don't confuse standing up for yourself with displeasing your grandmother. They aren't mutually exclusive ideas. If we want to be friends, we'll be friends. It's up to us, not Tansy."

Anna glanced at him, sitting there with his dark hair rakishly tousled, looking so handsome and solid and good, every woman's dream. Well, not every woman's, obviously, but hers. Definitely her dream. And he had just offered her some sort of friendship. That was better than nothing. Was she going to let Tansy take it away from her? Reeves was right about doing what was best for herself, and she would, just on her own terms. As soon as she figured out how exactly to accomplish that.

In the meantime, this evening was the closest thing she'd ever had to a date with Reeves, and it might be as close as she ever got to one. She intended to enjoy it.

They talked for hours. When they finally discussed the dossier he had given her, she found herself admitting that she was a bit uncertain about sticking her neck out.

"Dennis is at least a known quantity," she pointed out. "How do I know the next situation will be any better?"

"You just have to have faith."

He told her about the disaster of his marriage, bringing Anna to conclude, "Marissa wasn't who you thought she was."

"Believe me, I realize that," he said. "The thing is, how do you trust your own judgment again after you've made such a mistake?"

"Someone recently told me that you just have to have faith," Anna answered.

"Ouch. Coming back to bite me." He grinned and slid

toward the edge of the booth. "Well, now that we've cleared that up, I have a house to inspect tonight. Come on, I'll give you the ten-dollar tour."

"You'll have to put it on my account," Anna quipped.

Reeves laughed as he stood. Curious and reluctant to let the evening end, she followed suit. She just hoped Tansy didn't find out that she'd spent this time with Reeves; otherwise, she'd never hear the end of it. Tansy would forever remind her how she'd blown her one chance, however remote, to have her dreams fulfilled. She would never understand that it was as much her own fault as Anna's. Then again, what did it matter? Her relationship with her grandmother had never been what she'd wanted it to be anyway. It was too late, surely, to do anything about that now.

It was nearing ten o'clock when Reeves once again pulled into the driveway of his house. A motion detector set off a light that illuminated the drive and walkway out front, all the way to the mailbox on the street, reminding him that he hadn't checked the mail yet. Having called Chatam House earlier to say good-night to Gilli and been assured by Aunt Mags that all was well on their end, he felt no need to rush. In fact, he felt a great reluctance to let the evening end.

He had never talked so easily with anyone else or felt so… not comfortable exactly. Some of his thoughts and impulses about Anna were becoming increasingly uncomfortable. Yet, tonight with her he'd felt a certain rightness, a kind of confidence about himself and his personal life that had been missing previously.

Funny, he'd never had any trouble when it came to business and his career, but when it came to his personal relationships, he'd always been somewhat uncertain. That ought to come as no surprise, considering his parents' history. He realized now that he couldn't know what he hadn't been taught, but God had provided some very valuable lessons of late, and he meant to put them to good use.

Punching the button overhead, he waited for the garage door to lift, then pulled the sedan inside before hurrying around to hand Anna out on her side.

"Hang on a minute, will you?" he said by way of excusing himself.

Leaving Anna standing, he loped out to the curb, where he drew a handful of papers from the dark interior of the mailbox. He glanced over them on his way back up the drive, finding an electric bill among the advertising circulars, along with a letter. Looking at Marissa's name on the return address, he sighed inwardly, but the old familiar burn of failure did not come.

He didn't realize that he'd halted his steps until the motion detector clicked off the decorative lamp affixed to the brick on the corner of the house, leaving only the light from the garage to illuminate the envelope in his hand. This, he told himself with surprising serenity, was his past. Looking up at Anna, the thought occurred to him that there might well stand his future, and suddenly he wanted to run toward it. Her. Them. Yes, them. Him and Anna. Together. If only she didn't let Tansy get in the way.

Setting off with long, sure strides, he slid Marissa's letter and the other mail into his jacket pocket. Anna had been studying the bare, half-empty interior of his garage with probing intensity, as if the trash cans, tools and lawnmower in the corner might tell her what she would find inside the house. As he drew near, she looked around at him.

He'd kissed her before and had wanted to since then. Something must have warned her, for she drew back a step, asking, "What?"

"This," he said. Taking her beautiful face in his hands, he drew her to him even as he stepped closer to her and bent his head.

He risked everything on that kiss, blending his lips with hers in gentle urgency banked with a need far deeper than he'd realized and a joy he had not even suspected.

Yes, he thought. Yes. Yes. Yes.

Oh, but he could be a slow, foolish man! All these years, not to realize who and what he had in her.

He did a very thorough job with the kiss. When he had made all of it that he could, he wrapped his arms around her, holding her close to his heart, while it pounded and he got his breath back.

"Thank You," he whispered, eyes shut tight.

"What for?"

The light had gone off, the timer having run out, so that they stood in the dark now. He chuckled and turned her face up with a hand spread beneath her chin, trying to make out her expression.

"I wasn't talking to you." The whites of her eyes gleamed, widening. He felt the urge to kiss her again but didn't, knowing that it would not be wise, and he wanted to be wise this time, very, very wise. He loosened his embrace, turning her toward the door in the back wall. "Come on."

Turning on lights as they went, they entered the house through a short passageway open on one side to the kitchen, with the laundry room off the other and the master bedroom at the end. He led her there by the hand. Moving swiftly in through one side of the room, they peeked into the spacious master bath and large closets, then went out the other door into another hallway that soon opened onto the large living area of the great room. She admired the free-standing fireplace that separated living and dining spaces, as well as the study that opened off the opposite wall through glass-fronted French doors. Nearly everything had been covered and taped in preparation for painting, giving the place a ghostly, unreal quality.

He showed her Gilli's frilly pink gingham room and the

nanny's room, along with two other bedrooms before pulling down the attic stairs and climbing up to poke his upper body through the opening and take a look around. The place looked clean and new. The ceilings had all been replaced, along with the insulation atop them, and everything below had at last been taped, bedded and plastered. Only some sanding and the painting remained to be done. It was as if the honeybees had never invaded.

They walked around past the dining area, with its gleaming brass chandelier hanging shrouded over the center of the canvas-draped table and on to the formal entry. It was nothing so grand as Chatam House, of course, but the architect had carved out space enough for an exquisite Louis XVI console table, along with a matching bench and framed mirror, which had been the aunties' wedding gifts to him and Marissa. It was only here, in this forward space, where the ceiling had not had to come down, so the furnishings remained uncovered.

Anna ran a hand over the marble top of the table, sighing with pleasure. "I've always loved old things. Guess it has to do with growing up in an old house."

He considered a moment then asked the question now uppermost in his mind. "Think you'd like living in a new house, say, this house?"

She shot him an uncertain look, folding her cardigan close. "This is a wonderful house," she answered carefully. "You can't imagine how far beyond my dinky old apartment it is or you wouldn't even ask me that."

"We both know that's not what I'm asking."

He leaned a hip against the table and pressed his hands to his thighs. Why wasn't his heart pounding? he wondered. It had pounded like a big brass drum every time he'd broached, however obliquely, the subject of a possible future with Marissa. How could he now feel so calm, after the spectacular failure of his marriage to Marissa and his initial opinion of Anna?

Anna-Miranda-the-Brat-Burdett.

The old refrain sang through his head, childish voices chanting. As if she'd heard them, too, her head came up, her gaze meeting his. Wide and troubled, her sky-blue eyes had never seemed so sad. She shook her head.

"If you'd said anything like that even a couple days ago, I think I'd have jumped over the moon."

He didn't know if that was a good start or a bad one. Draping an arm across her shoulders, he pulled her around to lean beside him. "And now?" She shook her head again, looking away. "It's not Tansy, is it?" he asked.

"You tell me."

"You can't think this is about her money."

"No, but something's put this in your head."

"You," he said. "It's you.

Sighing, she let him see her worry. "That's just it, Reeves. I'm not sure I know how to live a normal life. My whole life's been about fighting Tansy. I don't know how to do anything else."

He tugged her closer. She leaned her head on his shoulder. It was a nice feeling, a good feeling, a *right* feeling.

"We've been living normal lives, Anna, both of us. This is what the world offers. I think it's time we started living the lives God means for us to have." He laid his cheek against the top of her head. "Let's give it some time, see what He has in store for us. The auction is weekend after next. Let's get through that and see where we are then? Okay."

For answer, Anna shifted and slid both of her arms around his waist. They stayed there like that for several long, sweet moments, until at last she whispered, "Why couldn't Tansy stay out of it?"

"Just put Tansy out of your mind," he told her with some exasperation. "Now, about the auction. Parking's going to be a premium. I could send the aunties' car for you, but I have the feeling Chester is going to have his hands full. Why don't I—"

She pulled back, frowning. "What are you talking about? Why would you send a car? I'm not going to the auction."

"Of course, you're going. How could you not go?"

"I'm not on the guest list."

"That doesn't matter. I didn't get an invitation, either, but I've already had my tux dry-cleaned because I know that my aunts would never forgive me if I wasn't there."

"That's different."

"No, it isn't."

"You're family," she pointed out.

He couldn't believe this. Surely she realized how much his aunts adored her. They would definitely want her there. He wanted her there. He had, in fact, intended to take her as his date, but he could see that would not do. Tansy would undoubtedly be in attendance, and that in itself would give Anna enough reason not to accompany him. Folding his arms, he took the only tack available to him.

"I can't believe you would intentionally offend my aunts this way."

"You know that's not—"

"Hypatia in particular will be very hurt. She already thinks you blame her and the other aunts for Tansy's manipulations."

"I never said that."

"What else are they to think?" He demanded, throwing up his hands for good measure.

Looking resigned, she sighed. "If you really believe I should go…"

"I know it."

She made a face. "All right. I'll put in an appearance, at least."

"That would be best," he told her, somehow managing to keep a straight face and not break out in a relieved grin.

"But I'll get there under my own power," she informed him smartly. Shooting him a resentful glare, she muttered, "Now I have to find something to wear."

He almost told her to be sure to wear those classy heels but bit back the words at the last moment.

"If you'll excuse me," she said, acid dripping from every syllable, "I have to go look through my closet now."

Hiding a smile, he let her out through the front door and walked with her to her coupe at the curb, where he offered her the briefest of goodbyes. Standing back, he watched her get in and drive away. Only when the red glow of her taillights disappeared from sight did he turn back to the house, grinning widely.

It was a nice house, he thought, looking up at the brick and stone facade, but it would be nicer still with her inside it. He could only pray that, whatever happened next, she would eventually feel the same way.

The invitation arrived at the print shop the first thing Monday morning, hand-delivered by the Chatams' houseman and driver Chester. With it came a second invitation and an apologetic note from Hypatia, saying that the extra invitation was for Dennis and his wife. Well, Anna thought, that ought to appease her cranky boss a bit. She still wasn't happy about having to attend the fund-raiser, partly because she'd had to come up with an outfit to wear but mostly because Reeves and Tansy would be there. She could already feel Tansy watching her every move. Every word, every gesture, ever glance would be watched and weighed, especially if Reeves was involved, and he would be.

She'd spent two sleepless nights thinking about Reeves's *suggestion.* She wouldn't think of it as an almost-proposal. She'd go mad if she allowed herself to imagine, even for a moment, that he might have been sincere. He couldn't be. He just could not be. She didn't know how to deal with the possibility that he might.

More than once, she'd tried to pray about it, but something stopped her. It was as if something blocked her, something at which she didn't want to look too closely. Perhaps that was because she knew that what was stopping her from taking her problems to God did not come from Him. Something in her got in the way, something she couldn't bring herself to face even now. Facing Reeves again, while she wasn't looking forward to it, seemed easier by comparison. Facing Tansy, well, that was just same old same old.

Surprisingly, Tansy had not shown up on her doorstep over the weekend to complain about her dinner plans going awry, but she would do so. It was just a matter of time. Of much more concern was the echoing silence from the direction of Reeves Leland. A girl could be excused for thinking that a guy who *suggested* to the point of almost proposing would call, couldn't she? Even if she had almost turned him down.

If only he had beat Tansy to the punch, if he'd come to his "understanding" of her before Tansy had tried her heavy hand at matchmaking, if he'd given her any indication that he might actually love her, then she would be the happiest woman in the world. But once again, Tansy had ruined it. Yet, Anna could not prevent herself from hoping and waiting for that phone to ring. When it finally did on Saturday morning, Reeves was not the one she heard.

"Anna?" Gilli's piping little voice was unmistakable. "Me and Special miss you."

Anna's heart turned over. "I'm sorry, sweetie."

"Ever'one's too busy to play," Gilli complained. "They got swings and slides at the park," she added hopefully.

Reeves took the phone then. "Sorry to put you on the spot," he said to Anna, "but it's a madhouse over here. Gilli's hoping you'll meet her in the park, get her out of the way for a while."

What could Anna say but, "Of course. I'd be delighted."

"Is half an hour too soon?" The poor man sounded desperate. No doubt the Chatam sisters had him running himself ragged with preparations for the fund-raiser.

"Not at all. In fact, I'm leaving now."

Gilli cheered when he related that news to her. Anna grabbed her keys. Not fifteen minutes later, she parked her car near the playground down the hill from the century-old Chautauqua building, where the community supported cultural activities such as plays, chamber music concerts and the occasional ballet performance and art show. Reeves and Gilli had already arrived and were walking across the grass toward the graveled playground, where several other children ran and laughed in the cool spring sunshine. Hailing them, Anna ran down the hill to sweep Gilli into an exuberant hug.

"What do you want to do first?"

"Swing!"

They ran to the swings hand in hand. Anna helped Gilli get situated and started her moving before turning to Reeves. He looked achingly handsome in jeans and a creamy tan pullover. She was prepared to tell him that she'd have Gilli back to the house before her nap time, but instead of heading off toward his car, as she'd expected, he ambled close enough to say, "Thanks for coming. I didn't think I'd ever get her out from underfoot. Didn't want to leave her cat. I had to bribe her with you."

Anna blinked as he stepped around her and gave Gilli a little shove that had her giggling with glee. "Don't you have to get back?" Anna asked him.

"Nope. Not until after lunch. Where were you thinking of eating, by the way?"

"I wasn't—" Anna began, only to be interrupted by Gilli yelling, "Pizza!"

"No pizza," Reeves said flatly, giving Gilli another shove. She put her head back and laughed as the swing flew a few feet higher. "How about that new deli on the square?" he asked Anna. "I hear they have good sandwiches and salads. Have you been there yet?"

"Uh, no, but—"

"Let's do that, then." He turned his attention back to Gilli, saying, "Hold on tight, sugar. This one's going to touch the sky."

He pushed her hard enough to elicit a squeal of delight. When he refused to go any higher, however, she quickly decided that it was time to hit the slides.

"Come on, Anna," she cried, racing off as soon as her feet touch the ground.

Anna glanced at Reeves then followed, and so it went until Reeves declared it time for lunch. Even with her stomach growling, Gilli resisted until Anna promised, "We'll come back soon."

"She'll remember that, you know," Reeves warned, taking Anna's hand, "and if she doesn't, I will."

Anna didn't know what to say to that, so she merely smiled, her heart swelling. There was some reason why this was not a good idea, but she couldn't for the life of her remember what it was until they were leaving the deli nearly an hour later and ran into a friend of her grandmother's. The speculation in that older woman's eyes told Anna that Tansy would know about this outing before she could even get back home.

She waited all day, after taking her leave of Reeves and a yawning Gilli, for that knock on her door, but it never came. Bucking up her courage to attend church again the next day, she told herself that Tansy would surely confront her there. Once more, however, she missed her guess. Tansy did walk by after Reeves sat down on the pew beside Anna, but she literally turned her head away without saying a word. Certain this was some new tactic of her grandmother's, Anna could barely concentrate on the sermon for trying to figure out what her response should be. Noticing her distraction, Reeves asked if she wanted to go somewhere and talk after the service, but Anna feared that was the last thing she should do. She couldn't think with him standing so close and smiling like that.

"I—I'm sorry. I can't."

A look of disappointment on his face, he took her hand in his, sweeping his thumb across her knuckles. "You won't stand me up next weekend, will you, Anna? My aunts want you at that auction, and they'll be so disappointed if you're not there."

"I'll be there!" she promised, but he called almost nightly to make sure, and more often than not, they wound up talking for hours.

She learned about his work and his company, his many siblings—six kids spread about among five parents!—and how responsible he felt, as the oldest, for the difficulties that divorce had caused them.

"And here I am repeating the same mistake," he said with a sigh.

"That's not your fault," she told him.

"Of course, it's my fault," he refuted softly. "I picked Marissa, for all the wrong reasons, but I've learned my lesson, believe me. I'll get it right next time."

Anna blanched to think of him marrying some other woman, but she quickly changed the subject. That didn't keep her from thinking about it, though, and when Saturday finally came, she took more pains with her appearance than she ever had before. Let Tansy crow. For once, Anna just didn't care.

Chapter Fourteen

Reeves paced the foyer impatiently. The soft strains of music, produced by a piano and harp, blended with the clink of flatware as the temporary staff put the final touches on the tables in the ballroom. Where was she? A good many guests had arrived already, and Anna had promised to be early. He should have insisted on picking her up.

Stationed in front of a narrow window, Chester opened the door. Reeves whirled and saw Tansy Burdett, decked out in matronly gray silk, enter.

She smiled thinly. "Not arrived yet, has she?"

Reeves took a stranglehold on his temper. "Stay away from her, Tansy. Just give her some room tonight, will you please?"

"I know my part in this," she huffed, marching toward him.

"That's just it. You have no part."

To his surprise, her chin wobbled. "I'll always have a part in my granddaughter's life," she insisted in a trembling voice, "even if it's from a distance. She's all I have."

Before Reeves could follow up on that, Chester announced, "She's here, Mr. Reeves."

Tansy marched away at double-time. His mouth dry and

palms damp, Reeves faced the door. He gave his French cuffs a tug and rolled his shoulders beneath the black satin-trimmed jacket of his tux. With a black bow tie and a white cummerbund against a white shirt, he suddenly felt colorless and trite. Chester swung that door open, and Reeves ceased to think at all.

It was just a long, slim midnight-blue skirt of some slinky knit, slit to the knee on one side, and a sleeveless, fitted, purple lace top worn beneath a length of sheer dark blue fabric draped over her shoulders and arms, but it looked as fine on her as any ball gown. She'd tucked her hair behind her ears and clipped rhinestones—or whatever they called faux diamonds these days—to her dainty lobes. A matching string encircled her slender neck and one wrist. On her feet were those delightful shoes. Wow.

Summoning up what he hoped to pass off as charm and wit, he stepped forward and shook his head, saying, "Oh, this is not good."

She looked down at herself in alarm. "What?"

"How will anyone concentrate on the auction items with you in the room?" She laughed, taking the arm he offered. "You're stunning," he told her softly, "beautiful, and if you get farther than three feet away from me tonight, I won't be responsible for my actions." She laughed again, a bright, crystalline tinkle that sounded like happiness itself.

They strolled toward the ballroom, passing half a dozen flower arrangements on pedestals. "Where's Gilli?" she asked.

"Oh, she's around here somewhere. I told her she could mingle until dinner started, provided she's on her best behavior. Then Carol will take her to the kitchen for a private party with Special. We can slip off and put her to bed afterward."

Anna nodded and squeezed his arm. "I'd like that."

The aunties were at their stations, Odelia at the door to greet, Mags directing guests to the proper seats, Hypatia handing out catalogs and pointing out items displayed on the rectangular tables that lined the room. The round tables, decorated in layers of white and gold, that stood in the center of the floor were for dining. With flickering candles on every table and an abundance of flowers, the room resembled a fairy glade, an impression enhanced by the smattering of light reflected upon the ceiling and the faint, ethereal lilt of the music.

He knew a moment of tension when Anna spied Tansy bending over one of the bid sheets on the display tables. As if sensing her presence, Tansy straightened and looked straight at them, but then she went back to penning in her bid, and Anna turned away. Reeves said nothing, smoothing a hand over her back until she relaxed.

The evening progressed smoothly from that point. He and Anna made the rounds of the auction tables and dutifully made bids on various items. One of them, a trip to the Bahamas donated by a local travel agency, was proving extremely popular, but Reeves made a generous bid anyway, imagining Anna and himself on the beach. She chose small, inexpensive items and made modest bids, which he upped at every opportunity in hopes of being able to present one or more of them to her.

Every chair was filled by the time dinner was served, and the bid sheets, according to his aunt's whispered progress reports, were nicely covered. They were on track to raise a record-breaking amount for the scholarship fund.

Reeves recognized Anna's corpulent boss and his equally bountiful wife seated at another table across the room, as requested, but after a single wave, Anna paid them no more mind, nor they her. It was just as well. If he had his way, Reeves would keep her entirely to himself tonight.

The aunties had provided their guests with filets mignon, creamy scalloped potatoes with asparagus and a dish of sweet shredded carrots cooked with currants. For dessert, they were presented with chocolate mousse and a "nut mélange in a caramel glaze." If that didn't open wallets, Reeves didn't know what would. As soon as he was finished eating, he made a dash over to place one more bid on that Bahamas vacation, then he grabbed Anna by the hand and swept her from the room. It was time to put Gilli to bed. Chester met him in the hall, however, a grave, apologetic look on his face.

"You're needed in the parlor, Mr. Reeves, and I think the misses will want to be there, too."

"Is it Gilli?" Reeves asked, but Chester was already moving into the ballroom. Glancing at Anna, he clasped her hand tighter and tugged her swiftly toward the front of the house. Striding into the room, Anna at his heels, he swept it with his gaze, and came to a frozen halt.

Marissa sat on the settee, clad in a strapless, red spandex sheath that hugged her curves and ended at her ankles, where the straps of her black spike-heeled sandals began. Her legs crossed, she bobbed one foot impatiently. Gilli, dressed in ruffles and petticoats, perched on the very edge of the cushion beside her. They had the same hair, Reeves noted inanely, though Marissa had tamed her curls into bouncy waves that framed her face and tumbled about her shoulders.

The aunties arrived at about the same instant that Gilli let her feet slide down to the floor. "Hello, Daddy," she said with false cheer, her mouth curved into the parody of a smile. "Hello, Anna. Look who come."

The sly look on Marissa's face made his stomach turn over. Knowing that this sudden appearance could not be good, he mentally kicked himself for not having bothered to read that letter upstairs, though he doubted it would have made much difference in the end.

He started forward grimly, intending to haul Marissa out of there for a private conference, but the moment he stepped off, Gilli said, "She my mommy."

Reeves stopped immediately, realizing that the last thing his daughter needed was another ugly scene. He made himself relax and almost at once felt the steadying touch of Anna's hand just above the small of his back. As if in ugly parody, Marissa reached over and slid a hand down Gilli's fragile spine. Smirking, she looked up at him, the light of challenge in her hazel eyes.

"Sugar," Reeves said, smiling at his daughter, "why don't you check on Special? I'm sure he's missing you?"

"Okay, Daddy," she said, skipping around the table as if on her way to play.

"And while you're at it," he added, "take the aunties with you. They have guests to see to."

Marissa pursed her mouth, and smoothed a hand over her skirt. Reeves suspected that she had expected to be invited to join the gala evening. She had enough nerve to pull off something like that.

The aunties hustled out after Gilli, throwing him sorrowful, worried glances as they disappeared. Anna's hand never left his back. Somehow, he had not expected it to. Marissa folded her arms and did a lazy perusal of the antiques in the room. He could almost see the numbers clicking in her head as she judged their value. At the same time, he sent a prayer heavenward.

Help me, Lord. Whatever You're doing now, help me get my part right, for my little girl's sake.

"I thought I'd find you here in the lap of luxury," Marissa said with a smirk. "I notice you still haven't moved back into our house."

"My house," he corrected.

Ignoring that, she pointed her chin at Anna. "Who's this?"

He answered succinctly. "Anna. Why?"

Marissa shrugged. "Can't help wondering if she's after my home, that's all."

"You lost all right to that house when you walked out on

me and our daughter," Reeves said flatly. "It says so in the divorce decree."

She looked around pointedly. "Mmm, yes, well, you obviously have no need for it. I made a mistake not fighting for my fair share. I just felt so bad at the time." She slanted a smug look at Anna. "Breaking your heart like that and all."

A bark of laughter escaped him. "I kinda got over it."

"You won't get over losing your daughter," she snapped, her expression hardening.

Anna gasped and stepped up beside him. Reeves shifted his weight toward her, both as a warning and a comfort. He knew what Marissa wanted, and it wasn't Gilli, though she was not beneath using the child against him. Strangely, he was not afraid.

"Marissa," he said conversationally, "are you threatening to sue for custody of my daughter if I don't hand over my house to you?"

She picked at an invisible piece of lint on her skirt. "I'm told, by an attorney to whom I'm *very* close, that mothers almost always win in court."

So she had a new boyfriend, a lawyer. Reeves smiled, refusing to be rattled. "Is that so?"

Marissa sat back, folding her arms. "So, which will you give me, your daughter or the house?"

Before Reeves could say a word to that, Anna exclaimed, "The house! We'll give you the house."

Reeves looked at her in stunned wonder. Did she even know what she'd just said? "We?"

"A family is worth more than brick and stone," she argued, and the agonized look in her eyes said that she, above all others, knew it only too well. "Besides," she went on desperately, "it's not like she's going to live in it. She only wants to sell it."

Marissa sniffed. "Live in that pedestrian little bungalow? I don't think so. Even you had sense enough to move in here. Still, it will bring a pretty penny on the market."

Reeves didn't look at her. He was smiling at Anna, who was revealing her heart to him, all unknowing. "But where will we live, sweetheart?" he asked deliberately. "Your apartment's not big enough for the three of us."

"I don't know!" Anna exclaimed, grabbing fistfuls of his shirt. "I don't care. We'll live in a cardboard box, if we have to, but we can't put Gilli through a custody battle, no matter how it comes out in the end."

Reeves thought his heart would burst from his chest, if his face didn't split first. "You know you just agreed to marry me, don't you?"

"What? No! I—I mean…" She gulped, her eyes widening, and then she squared her shoulders and said, "Yes."

Cupping her face in his hands, he laughed, and said, "I love you, Anna Miranda Burdett."

She blinked. "You do?"

"You and Gilli matter more to me than anything else in this world," he told her, "certainly more than a heap of brick and mortar. But what about your grandmother?"

Anna looked up into his eyes and smiled tearfully. "I'd already decided that I couldn't let her get in the way of this. I've been in love with you for too long! Since high school, at least!"

Reeves beamed. "I know." Wrapping his arms around her, he pulled her close. "If only I'd known it at the time."

"Can't imagine how you missed it, Stick," she burbled against his chest. "What other girl went around gluing your keys to your locker?"

They looked at each other and burst out laughing.

Cupping her face, he put his forehead to hers. "Praise God," he said. "Finally, I got it right."

"How touching," Marissa remarked sourly.

Reeves pulled his gaze from Anna's, dropped his hands, slid his arm about his beloved's waist and looked to his glowering ex. "You can have the house," he told her, "under one condition." She raised an eyebrow, waiting for it. "You will allow Anna to adopt Gilli. Barn door's closed, Marissa. No more coming back to the trough."

Narrowing her eyes at him, she rose languidly to her feet. "Fine." But she couldn't resist sweeping her gaze over Anna and sneering, "I figured you'd go for the kid. You have that mousy housewife look about you."

Anna, to her credit, simply smiled. "What do you think, darlin'?" she asked him. "Do I look like your wife and Gilli's mother?"

"Oh, yeah. Most beautiful thing I've ever seen."

She kissed him, once, hard, on the lips.

Marissa tossed her head and slinked across the room, sniping, "I'll have my guy contact you."

"You do that," Reeves said, "but you get zip until those adoption papers are signed." He grinned down at Anna. "From now on, Gilli's going to have a real mother."

"And you are going to have a real wife," Anna promised softly.

Just then, Gilli burst into the room, the cat dangling from the crook of her arm. Marissa, who was near the door, shot Reeves a look of pure spite then bent to bring her face near Gilli's.

"I'm so sorry, Gilli," she droned, "but I won't be your mommy anymore. Your daddy—"

Before she could complete whatever malicious statement she'd been about to make, Gilli shoved her, declaring, "I don't want you!" With that she ran, not to Reeves, to Anna. "Wanna hold my cat?" she asked, gazing up at Anna adoringly.

Anna, fortunately, knew better than to even try such a thing. "I'd rather hold both of you," she said, scooping up Gilli, cat and all. Gilli giggled and reached out a hand to cup Reeves's cheek, letting him know that she approved of what was happening.

As Reeves turned his head to put a kiss in the center of that little palm, a throat cleared. He looked around to find Marissa gone and his aunts standing abreast in the doorway. Mags snuffled and wiped her eyes on her sleeve, while Auntie Od blew her nose into a lacy hanky. Even Hypatia's eyes sparkled with moisture, but she merely lifted her chin.

"There will be no cardboard boxes," she pronounced, shamelessly revealing that they had eavesdropped every word. "Not so long as Chatam House can offer the barest refuge."

Smiles and laughter erupted as the aunties rushed forward, babbling about weddings and what beautiful children they expected Anna and Reeves to make. Grinning, Reeves encircled his family with his arms, cat and all, his chest to Anna's back. With his chin snugged against her temple, he let the three most wonderful old dears in existence tell him about God's will for his life, just as if he didn't already hold it in his arms.

"Thank You," he whispered.

Anna put her head back and smiled before she lifted her gaze heavenward. "Me, too," she said. "Me, too."

Epilogue

Hypatia watched Anna dip a finger in icing then dab it onto the tip of Reeves's nose, laughing.

"Brat!" he growled over the fork with which he was trying to feed her a bite of their wedding cake. She was still laughing when he poked the cake into her mouth. With the other hand, he swiped the icing from his nose, and then, while Anna chewed, he smeared the remnants across her mouth. Swooping down, he kissed it away, to the applause and laughter of the guests gathered in the ballroom of Chatam House for the wedding reception.

Hypatia sighed. As beautiful a bride as Anna made in a floor-length, long-sleeved closely fitted sheath of Brussels lace, Reeves had never looked finer. He was not just the most handsome groom she had ever seen, he was also the happiest, most relaxed and confident. Gilli looked like a confection in her flower girl's dress, even with Special trotting at her ankles and trying to rub off the pink bow tied around his neck. In a break with tradition, Myra had served as ring bearer, with the rest of Reeves's siblings performing various other duties.

To everyone's relieved puzzlement, Tansy had not taken a large role in planning the event. She had, however, insisted on paying the cost of the hastily thrown together wedding. One could never tell with Tansy, though, which was why Hypatia stiffened when she saw the other woman march up to the happy couple with her shoulders back and her chin high.

"I have a gift," she announced, shoving a fat envelope into Reeves's hands.

Glancing warily at Anna, he opened the flap and took out the papers, unfolding them to study. After a moment, he looked up at Anna. "It's the deed to Burdett House."

Tansy lifted her chin higher still, ignoring Anna's gasp. "It's not Chatam House, but it has a long and gloried history." She fixed Anna with a steely gaze, adding, "And room enough for a large family."

Hypatia could see the war going on inside of Anna, and so could Tansy. "I've bought a little house on the other side of town, and I've already moved in. Burdett house would be yours one day, anyway," she told Anna. "Who else would I leave it to? You're all I've got." Her chin wobbled, but she went on gamely. "I know I've been hard on you, too hard, maybe, but it's because I was so soft with your father. After my husband died, I indulged Jordan. I made every excuse in the book for him." She squeezed her eyes shut and her voice cracked when she said, "I'm the reason he died of a drug overdose. He thought life was one long party, and I let him think it." Gulping, she looked at Anna. "I vowed not to make the same mistake with you. So instead I made others."

Anna bit her lip and looked to her husband of some two hours. Would moving into the house give Tansy a way to control them? Then again, would a man who hadn't blinked an eye at Tansy's money allow such interference? Anna apparently knew the answer to that question.

"It is a wonderful old house," she said with a slow smile.

Reeves folded the papers and stuck them back in the envelope. "The antiques that my aunts have given us would look good in it," he allowed, sending a pointed glance at Hypatia. She sent another back to him. No, she had not known what Tansy was planning, but she could find no grounds for objection to Tansy giving her house away, especially as it seemed to signal a great turnaround in Tansy's relationship with her granddaughter.

Reeves stashed the envelope in a pocket of his tuxedo and addressed Tansy, one arm pulling Anna close. "Thank you."

To everyone's surprise, Tansy's face crumpled and she began to cry. "Thank you!" she wailed. "All I've ever wanted is for her to be happy, and now she is!" She looked at Anna, tears sliding down the crevices in her face. "I knew how badly I'd messed up when you almost let him get away just to keep from pleasing me!"

Reeves and Anna exchanged looks, and then, as one, stepped forward to lightly embrace and pat Tansy. Gilli rushed over then, that confounded Special now clutched in the bend of her elbow. She tugged sharply on the tail of Tansy's stylish silk suit jacket.

"Wanna hold my cat?"

Tansy actually bent down to comply, and wonders of wonders, Special complacently allowed Tansy to drape him over her shoulder. Gilli followed them to a quiet corner, where they petted the cat and chattered happily.

Hypatia laughed, gazing with satisfaction at her nephew and his lovely wife. Just look, she thought, at all that God had done.

And just think of what He would yet do.

* * * * *

Want to read more about the aunts and their adventures in matchmaking?
Look for book two in the
CHATAM HOUSE *series,*
coming in Spring 2010,
only from Steeple Hill Love Inspired!

Dear Reader,

Even the most yielded Christians experience failure. It's part of life. Do you learn from failure? Does your self-esteem suffer when, despite your best efforts, the worst happens? Or have you learned that failure can be God's way of preparing us for something better than we have imagined?

Even the most yielded Christians experience emotional pain. Often, what hurts us just isn't fair or right. Sometimes we react in ways that, while entirely justifiable, may actually cause us more harm. Worse, we can become trapped by those "justifiable" actions and attitudes, causing much needless pain.

The "fix" for both difficulties is simple but profound: Jesus, in our hearts *and on our minds.* All the time. Think about it! Think about Him!

God bless,

Arlene James

QUESTIONS FOR DISCUSSION

1. Reeves and Gilli were driven out of their home by a massive infestation of honeybees—and straight into the sanctuary of Chatam House. In real life, does God ever use calamity to send us into sanctuary?

2. The failure of Reeves's marriage left him feeling inept and unloved, even by his three-year-old daughter. How did this affect his performance as a husband and father?

3. Anna rebelled at a young age out of blind resentment because of a feeling of emotional abandonment. Rebellion by children is often called "acting out" and acknowledged as normal, but it can have lifelong consequences. What could Anna's grandmother, Tansy, a Christian woman, have done to prevent Anna's rebellion from becoming a habit that tainted her whole life for many years?

4. What could lead a Christian woman to behave as Tansy did? Genuine concern? Emotional pain? A lack of faith? Misunderstanding of the parental or the Christian role?

5. According to Romans 3:6, "the mind controlled by the Spirit is life and peace." To Reeves, having a mind controlled by the Spirit meant dwelling on the things of Christ, rather than what had and could go wrong in his life. Do you agree or disagree with this outlook and why?

6. Reeves spoke about being "yielded" to the Holy Spirit. What does this mean? How is it accomplished? What benefits might be afforded the Christian who is truly

"yielded" to the Spirit? Complete freedom from worry? Recognition of God at work in one's life?

7. Is the fact that Anna prayed when she realized that she could be late for work after her run with Reeves significant? Why or why not?

8. Anna and Gilli seem to get along very well, despite Anna not being used to dealing with children. Why do you think this is?

9. Reeves came to consider Anna as the answer to his prayers. Why? Can one person be the answer to the prayers of another? Why or why not?

10. When did Reeves realize that Anna was no longer his enemy but someone he could spend the rest of his life with? Have you ever had someone in your life you thought you hated, but then fell in love with? How did it turn out?

11. The aunties not only discussed the possibility of a relationship between Reeves and Anna, they prayed about it and, at times, attempted to arrange for the two to bump into one another. Is this type of interference ever acceptable? Why or why not?

Private investigator Wade Sutton plans to hightail it out of Dry Creek long before December 25. The town holds too many *unmerry* memories. Until he's asked to watch over a woman in danger, a woman whose faith changes him forever.

Wade wished he had never come back to Dry Creek. Or, since he had come back, he wished people hadn't been so kind to him. Barbara making that cake for him was putting him off his game. And then Jasmine—usually he didn't have any trouble taking a tough line with a suspect. But then, he'd never been tempted to kiss a suspect before.

He watched Jasmine's back as she walked to the table. She was ramrod straight and angry with him. He knew he'd come on too strong, but it was either that or forgetting everything he knew about law enforcement and refusing to believe she could be responsible for anything.

As a lawman he had to consider all the possibilities, and it was hard to forget that Lonnie had been her partner. She could have sent him a coded message that in some way had helped him escape from prison, or at least given him an incentive to risk everything to get outside.

He wished he knew how to look into the heart of a person so he would know what Jasmine was thinking. Was she as innocent as she looked, or as guilty as she had been the first time she was convicted of a crime? He knew better than most how many ex-cons fell back into theft. He was often the one who took them in the second time around and listened to their sorry excuses.

"I gave you the biggest piece of cake," Barbara said as he sat down at his place at the table.

"Thank you." Wade smiled. It was the cake of his childhood fantasies, and he was going to have to force himself to eat it. All he wanted to do was take Jasmine home and then park his car at the end of the lane to her father's place. Why did she have to be tied up with Lonnie? Why couldn't she be a nice, ordinary woman like Barbara here? Carl never had to worry about arresting *her*.

Wade felt the smoothness of the cake on his tongue and the sweet tang of the raspberry filling. He smiled up at Barbara and thanked her again for the cake. The two kids at the table were smacking their lips and demanding more, just as Wade would be doing if he wasn't so troubled.

Then he looked down the table and saw his dear friend Edith. She wouldn't be happy about him keeping an eye on anyone. It was clear the older woman was very fond of Jasmine. That, of course, was the problem with being a lawman and trying to have friends. He liked things black and white with no shades of gray. He didn't want to have feelings for the suspect.

By doing his job, he was going to upset Jasmine and everyone else in Dry Creek. For the first time since he'd driven into town, he missed the barren feel of his apartment in Idaho Falls. He knew who he was there.

It didn't take long for Wade to leave the Walls' house, with Jasmine walking in front of him. The night was cold. Jasmine wrapped her arms around her body to keep warm and hurried to his car. He was still nursing that leg of his, so he went more slowly than she did. He made it in good time, though, and as he opened the car door for her, she nodded her thanks and slid into the passenger seat.

The first thing Wade did after he got into the car was to move the dial up on the heater. Snowflakes were just starting to fall, but they were scattered enough that he could clear them away with his windshield wipers.

He silently turned his car around and started down the sheriff's lane. The car lights shone on the falling snow, making the flakes look like pinpricks in the darkness.

"You don't think Lonnie would do something to my father, do you?" Jasmine asked. She looked up at him with eyes full of worry. "Lonnie's not very stable. I wouldn't want anyone around here to be hurt by him."

Wade shrugged. "With all you'd inherit if Elmer were out of the picture—"

Jasmine gasped. "I don't care about the money."

"Lonnie might."

That turned her quiet. He didn't want her to worry, though.

"He won't even have the chance to get close to anyone," Wade assured her. "We'll have the feds all over the place by tomorrow. Lonnie has a better chance of breaking in to Fort Knox than he has of sneaking into Dry Creek."

Wade hoped he wasn't lying. He had no idea what the feds would do. And they might have some completely different theories as to why Lonnie had broken out of prison. It might have nothing at all to do with Jasmine or anyone in Dry Creek.

"You'll be safe," Wade said as he opened his door.

He walked around to the passenger door and opened it. Wade stood by the open car door and watched as Jasmine pulled her coat closer to her body. She wasn't making any move to walk toward the house and he wasn't making any move to let her. Finally Wade reached out and touched her cheek. It was soft and a little damp. She must have been crying when she'd been huddled against the door on the drive out here.

"It'll be okay," he whispered to her as he brought his hand down.

"I'm fine," she said.

He nodded with a slight smile. "I know."

Wade had never kissed a suspect, but he would have done

it now if he hadn't thought it would make Jasmine cry even more. She was barely hanging on, and he needed to leave her with her dignity.

"I'll be parked at the end of Elmer's lane if you need me," Wade said as he stepped back from the door. Snow was falling in earnest now, but in his trunk he had a heavy sleeping bag that he used on stakeouts like this. "I'll come to the door in the morning, before I go over to my grandfather's."

"You can't sleep outside all night. It's freezing out here. I'll leave the kitchen door unlocked in case you need to come inside."

"Don't leave anything unlocked. I'll duck into the barn if I need to."

Jasmine nodded.

Wade watched her walk to the kitchen door and go inside the house. Only then did he head back to the driver's door. He wondered if he'd get any sleep tonight. He was losing his edge. The next thing he knew, he was going to be offering pillows to everyone he arrested and wishing them sweet dreams. When had he turned into a soft touch?

He waited for the light to go out in the kitchen before he started his drive down the lane. He already felt lonely.

* * * * *

Will Jasmine give Wade reason to call
Dry Creek home again?
Find out in
SILENT NIGHT IN DRY CREEK
by Janet Tronstad.
Available in October 2009
from Love Inspired®

TITLES AVAILABLE NEXT MONTH

Available September 29, 2009

SILENT NIGHT IN DRY CREEK by Janet Tronstad

Private investigator Wade Sutton plans to hightail it out of Dry Creek long before December 25th. Until he's asked to watch over a woman in danger, a woman whose faith could change him forever.

THE MATCHMAKING PACT by Carolyne Aarsen

After the Storm

Widowed rancher Silas Marstow's young daughter and her best friend are determined to see him and single mother Josie Cane married. *Very* determined!

THE PERFECT GIFT by Lenora Worth

Disoriented after a car crash, Goldie Rios wakes up on Rory Branagan's sofa. All Rory's sons want for Christmas is a new mom, but is this unexpected guest the mother they've been longing for?

BLUEGRASS CHRISTMAS by Allie Pleiter

Kentucky Corners

Desperate to unite a town in crisis through a good old-fashioned Christmas church pageant, Mary Thorpe tries to enlist handsome neighbor Mac McCarthy. But Mac's a holiday humbug. Can Mary bring the spirit of Christmas into his life—and love into his heart?

SOLDIER DADDY by Cheryl Wyatt

Wings of Refuge

Young Sarah Graham surprises everyone by passing U.S. Air Force commander Aaron Petrowski's nanny inspection. Only secrets in her past could destroy the home she's built in his heart.

DREAMING OF HOME by Glynna Kaye

Meg McGuire has unwittingly set her sights on the same job and house as single dad Joe Diaz. Determined to give his young son the best life he can, this military man isn't giving up without a fight. But soon Joe is dreaming of a home with the one woman who could take it all away.

LICNMBPA0909